EXIT, PURSUED BY A BARE

A serial killer hidden in plain sight

S.M. Sedgwick

The most needed support comes in the form of T.E.A.

Thank you all for being there.

'prō meīs nihil nōn patiar'

The author is a retired Detective Superintendent who it should be stressed bears no resemblance to his counterpart in this novel.

CONTENTS

PROLOGUE

It was an unusually warm day on which to celebrate his forty-seventh birthday, just as it had been thirty-three years earlier when he had committed his first murder.

His first victim had been carefully chosen and the plan had been executed with the precision of a seasoned veteran. He savoured the memory, replaying the episode in his mind as he had done countless times before. Sometimes he focused on one particular aspect but today was his birthday and he was feeling indulgent, today he would remember each delicious detail from the formation of the plan to its execution.

His office door was closed, the phone had been muted and he was standing in his favourite spot at the window. From the tenth-floor vantage point he had a panoramic view of the town, his town. The autumnal sun beat through the window in a determined effort to overcome the protective tint and he relished the warm glow that enveloped him. He closed his eyes to help focus on the memory but in truth there was no need as it remained as vivid as always.

Suddenly there was an urgent knock at the door and it was open before he could even command entry. He remained facing outward for a second to ensure his annoyance at the interruption was not transmitted to the junior staff member who was now several paces into his office.

"So sorry to bother you, sir, but Uniform are reporting a suspicious death in town," explained the Detective Sergeant in apologetic tones.

"Okay," he replied. "No rest for the wicked, eh?"

CHAPTER 1

Thirty-Three Years Ago

That particular summer had indeed been a hot one and for children on school holidays one gloriously sunny day seemed to endlessly roll into another. The quintessential English resort had changed little over the years; town planners and architects had seemingly accepted defeat in producing anything manmade to rival the perpetual majesty of the rugged coastline that stretched for miles either side of the town.

His victim had been a twelve-year-old boy and resident of a notorious children's home that was the scourge of the local residents and the Constabulary alike. Keith Hughes believed his first meeting with the older boy was entirely accidental. It happened a short time after he had enjoyed some rare good fortune whilst walking slowly back towards the children's home that evening, already two hours after his curfew. He had been holding a stick in his left hand and using it to casually rattle the railings of the boundary fence, as he walked past it. He ceased the irritating habit immediately upon seeing the wallet laying on the pavement, suddenly caring whether attention was drawn to his activity. After a furtive glance in each direction, he swiftly collected the article and put it in his trouser pocket almost without breaking stride. When out of public view around the corner and benefiting from the privacy of an unlit shop doorway, Keith checked the contents of the black leather wallet. His heartbeat quickened as he started counting the range of Bank of England notes now in his hands. Temporarily distracted by his sudden wealth, Keith failed to hear the soft footsteps approach. Suddenly he was lifted from the ground and thrown violently into the dark recess of the doorway that had previously been a welcome sanctuary from prying eyes.

"You thieving bastard," screamed the wild-eyed Paul Avery, following up his initial assault with a hard kick into Keith's midriff.

The youngster screamed in fear and then in pain as he felt the full impact of Avery's steel-capped right boot. Two more blows followed in quick succession until Avery felt he had established complete control over the now crying boy before him. Avery casually picked up his wallet that he had carefully placed on the pavement minutes earlier and meticulously counted the contents to ensure they were complete. He heard the boy whimper something about finding the money but chose to ignore the comments, preferring to allow the menace of his mere presence, standing above the boy, to suffice at that moment.

Although this was their first meeting, Avery knew Keith Hughes very well. He had carefully selected him, over a period of time observing him covertly whenever he could. He was the predator and Keith was the vulnerable prey that frequently left the security of his herd. He knew that Keith lived a solitary existence, distancing himself from the other residents of the home that was given a wide berth by the rest of the community. He suspected that Keith's days were filled with aimless daydreams and occasional petty crime as even though only a young teenager himself, Avery was already an advanced people watcher. The lad practically had the word 'victim' tattooed on his stupid freckled forehead.

Avery had guessed the boy would be easy to manipulate and after thirty minutes of mind play, Keith had virtually sold his soul to the older boy just to feel some pseudo-brotherly acceptance. And so, the unlikely relationship developed with the two boys meeting in secret locations most days and at each meeting Keith fell more and more under Avery's spell, culminating in that fateful September afternoon.

The boys had both lived in the tired seaside town all their lives. One in a Local-Authority-run home for 'unfortunates', a term invented and owned by the good people of the town, the other in a typical three-bedroomed semi with his parents. They were equally conversant with the geography of the area. Avery, however, was far more comfortable exploring the rugged coastline and isolated coves away from the bright and noisy amusement arcades preferred by his young protégé. Such was his eagerness to please, Keith tried hiding his reluctance to follow Avery as he clambered across the slippery rocks. Avery responded to the obvious difficulties of his shadow by going faster over the terrain and offering no encouragement to the boy. After nearly twenty minutes' relentless effort, Avery reached the ledge that provided a wonderful vantage point over the sea, some forty feet below. He had sat on this very ledge many times in the past. He could not have designed a better place than the one nature had provided for him. The overhanging rock shielded any view from the coastal road above and the sharp rocks combined with the notoriously treacherous tide, deterred most tourists from coming anywhere near the spot. In any case, the ledge provided clear views in either direction. Anybody coming would be spotted long before they saw him sitting amongst the natural camouflage of the rock face behind him. Best of all, was the relentless sound of the sea, directly below his swinging feet, as he sat on the very edge and watched the toiling Keith gradually getting closer to him. The younger boy was breathing heavily as he joined Avery on the ledge.

"See, I told you it was fantastic," enthused Avery.

The exertion of the climb caused Keith to respond more honestly than he had at the start of their journey.

"Is this it?" he asked, clearly unimpressed with the vantage point and its panoramic view. "I cut my knees on those bloody rocks," added the youngster, preferring to examine his superficial injuries rather than marvel at the wonder of Avery's 'special' place.

The boys sat in silence for a few moments, each thinking their own and very different thoughts, before Keith dared to venture a suggestion that they should climb back down. He provided what he believed to be a valid reason to Avery, that he was hungry. In truth, the combined sight of Avery's swinging legs and the expanse of water below was making the non-swimmer incredibly nervous, though the considerable depth of the ledge meant that he was able to sustain a semblance of bravado.

His sense of security immediately evaporated as Avery quietly replied, "We're not going down that way, we are going for a swim."

"What do you mean?" stammered Keith, hoping against hope that Avery would reassure him with a laugh to demonstrate he was joking.

Avery didn't laugh as he looked toward the horizon.

"You trust me, don't you Keith?"

"Yes, I guess," replied Keith with a quiet dread evident in his voice.

"Well, I'm a strong swimmer and have jumped off here loads of times. It's a brilliant feeling."

"But I can't swim," whimpered Keith who was shaking despite the warmth of the afternoon sun.

"Well, it's a good job that I'm training to be a lifeguard," replied Avery.

"Please Paul," was all Keith could manage to say as he suppressed the sobs that were moments away.

Avery laughed and pointed at the younger boy.

"Had you going there, sucker. Come on, let's climb down and go and get some chips."

Relief flooded through Keith's body as he gratefully accepted Avery's offer of an outstretched hand to help him to his feet.

The horror of his mistake was at least brief as Avery pulled him violently up and propelled him towards the edge, releasing his grip to prevent Keith's momentum from taking both boys to their death. Keith's scream was abruptly ended as he entered the cold water directly below the now singularly occupied ledge.

Avery saw the boy flounder for a few seconds when briefly surfacing from the unforgiving waves. He was genuinely fascinated by Keith's futile struggle for life as unseen forces pulled him back out of sight before showing tantalising glimpses of the last few seconds of the boy's existence. Avery knew there could be no escape as the sheer rock face at sea level prevented any egress from the water and wondered whether even a strong swimmer could have extricated himself from such a predicament. When there were no more sightings of the boy, Avery occupied himself by throwing stones into the vast expanse of sea before him. Then, as the light began to fade, he climbed down the rocks and retraced his steps to the coastal path the boys had walked along earlier.

On the way home, he bought some chips and saw a police car drive by. He was confident that the lack of blue lights and sirens meant there was no connection to events he had just orchestrated.

He was, however, fascinated by the car and its smart uniformed occupants who could clearly go where they wanted unchallenged. He waved at the officers causing them to smile and wave back confirming his decision that a career in the Constabulary would be an excellent life choice.

CHAPTER 2

Twenty Years ago

"You're a dead man, copper."

The rasped utterance from the darkened shop doorway was an unwelcome intrusion into the otherwise uneventful night shift for the station's newest recruit. Sebastian Bare felt that the noise of his pounding heart would drown out any radio transmission he might make, but the issue became irrelevant as his older colleague immediately offered his own retort to the threatening doorway.

"Don't be a wanker all your life, Jack."

Jack clearly took this as a standard form of greeting and shuffled from his doorway with a broad grin present, exposing a set of teeth that had clearly suffered from their owner's unconventional and nomadic lifestyle. The town's most infamous 'down and out' was clearly delighted to have introduced himself to a new member of the Constabulary in such an impactive way. He appeared genuinely surprised when the offer of his blackened, outstretched right hand was met with a look of disdain from PC Bare.

"Seb, meet Jackanory," said his colleague by way of introduction. "So called because he is the greatest story-teller to have ever lived in this area."

The smile reappeared on Jack's unshaven face, the grime of sustained street life patently evident despite the lack of lighting in the street that he had adopted as home that particular spring night. PC Bare, composure regained but with a heart rate still faster than he would have liked, listened with interest to the dialogue between his two companions. He wondered what stance his colleague would take against the obviously drunk but seemingly harmless individual.

His recollection of dealing with this type of encounter, in a staged training school scenario, was somewhat hazy and he hoped he wouldn't be tested as to his police powers in such situations by his tutor constable. Given the overpoweringly unpleasant odour that accompanied Jackanory's every movement, the young officer also hoped that any technique he was required to use wouldn't involve a search of his new-found friend. He was relieved that the conversation was clearly a common one between the two men and centred on an apparent genuine concern for the homeless one.

After the officers had resumed their slow-paced foot patrol of the town's deserted streets, PC Bare was provided with a life history of Jack by his tutor constable.

"He came to the town about the same time as me, around twenty years ago. God knows why he picked this place. I think it's where they kicked him off the train."

It emerged that Jack was around fifty years old, although he appeared considerably older. Initial hostility directed at him by the residents of the small town had dissipated over the years and been replaced by tolerance and even affection. He was the adopted hobo and had become as much of a feature as the ugly museum that contained little local heritage yet nevertheless was a compulsory visit for the town's reluctant Year 7 schoolchildren.

Jack was as inoffensive as an alcoholic who slept rough could possibly be. Whilst mothers didn't exactly encourage interaction with their children, they were not fearful if he attempted to entertain their offspring with a story as he sat on the park's monument steps in the summer. If Jack's true identity had ever been known, it had long since been forgotten. He was happy to answer to the name the local Constabulary had bestowed upon him in tribute to the countless occasions he had volunteered himself as a vital witness in exchange for a warm cell and a hot drink. Strangely, Jackanory's self-promoted worth as a witness to serious crime coincided with the coldest winter nights, whereas in the summer, he rarely witnessed even the most minor misdemeanour.

Much to the young officer's initial consternation, Jack would often insist on walking alongside the patrolling officer during his foot patrols. The self-appointed tour guide liked his uniformed friend who appeared more receptive to his company than the vast majority of his colleagues. Bare tolerated the company and occasionally found himself buying a hot snack for the man. On his first Christmas duty he had even sought out the wandering storyteller and presented him with a bottle of scotch as a present. Jack had briefly taken the bottle but after inspection had returned it to the confused officer.

"I can't take this, son," he said apologetically.

"Why not?" asked the confused constable.

"Well don't take this the wrong way but when it comes to whiskey, I only ever drink the good stuff, it's a rule I will never break."

"Oh! Fair enough," said Bare, embarrassed that his rare act of philanthropy had turned so quickly into a social faux pas.

CHAPTER 3

Police Constable Avery stood in the deserted quarry not feeling the chill in the November night air. The remote location coupled with the early-hour time slot meant it was incredibly quiet. Well, that was if you discounted the muffled angry cries coming from the boot of the Ford Escort containing his prisoner Simon Vickers. Avery leant against the car and reflected on the events leading to this point. It had been a largely uneventful late shift and Avery had been walking back toward the police station in the latter stages of his lone foot patrol. He was due to finish at 11pm and a quick check of his illuminated wristwatch suggested he should slow his pace so as not to arrive early and risk adverse comment from his Sergeant. Not that he particularly cared about the view of his supervisor but more that he avoided those small details that got you noticed. It suited him to remain in the middle of the herd, camouflaged by a cloak of mediocrity at this stage of his career.

He therefore chose the slightly longer route for the last leg of his journey which took him along Talbot Road past the Mariners Arms Public House, the sole building left standing in a poor area of the town earmarked for an ambitious regeneration project. The pub itself was now boarded up and empty following a drugs raid at the premises earlier in the year. The planned development suited the

Constabulary as it had been an opportunity to permanently close a place that had been notorious as a haven for drug dealers over the years. The District Council had been equally pleased as it removed the last area of resistance to their ambitious redevelopment plans.

Avery was therefore surprised to see a vehicle parked in the small private car park adjacent to the pub. He walked across and saw the small dark Ford Escort was unattended. A touch of the car bonnet revealed it to be stone cold indicating the vehicle had been there a while. Avery was about to depress the transmit button on his radio to request a check on the Police National Computer when the car's owner appeared walking haphazardly into the car park. The intoxicated male was recognised immediately by Avery as being Simon Vickers.

The pair had last come into contact the previous week at the scene of a large disturbance at another notorious pub on the other side of town. Upon police arrival at the disturbance, Avery and his colleagues had managed to arrest the main antagonists and had led them handcuffed away through a baying crowd to a waiting police Transit van. Vickers, a petty drug dealer and thief, had been part of the crowd and whilst in close proximity to Avery had spat in the young officer's face. Due to the fact that Avery already had his hands full with a violent detainee he could do nothing about the attack apparently unwitnessed by his colleagues and watched Vickers melt into the crowd with a satisfied grin on his face.

There was no hint of mutual recognition on Vickers' face as he approached the officer standing next to his car. The combination of recently consumed drink and drugs had however given him the platform from which to question the authority of the uniform standing in front of him. Sober or not he was used to the ritual of verbally abusing the local Constabulary only to desist when arrest seemed more probable than not.

"Leave my car alone, pig," he said, producing marginally less spittle but in a less focused fashion than their last encounter.

Now Avery did not believe in fate but in that split second decided the coincidence of the encounter was too good an opportunity to pass on. Using the advantage of his weight, height and sobriety, Avery propelled Vickers' face first into the cold brick wall that surrounded the small car park. It had been easy to put his prisoner in a rear wrist lock and then restrain him further using a cable tie taken from his uniform jacket pocket. The cable ties that Avery and other officers carried were normally used as temporary restraints once handcuffs had already been used but on this occasion the officers' cuffs remained in their holster. A cursory search of Vickers' outer garments revealed the car keys to be in his trouser pocket. The officer was now only speaking in quiet controlled commands as he retrieved the keys.

"On your knees." The order was emphasised by a sharp dig into Vickers' ribs, who felt the indignation of his treatment more than the pain. His outrage grew further as from the kneeling position he was suddenly pushed face-down into the dirt and rubble. The dust in his mouth made his comments virtually inaudible but Avery thought he heard the word 'complaint' amongst the rhetoric. With supreme efficiency Vickers' ankles were also cable tied allowing the officer to unlock the car that was close to the prone and still protesting owner of it. Avery found an oily rag in the boot and was able to fashion it quickly into a gag. The confined boot area was largely empty, but it had still been a struggle to fill it with the hog-tied Vickers before slamming the lid shut and using the key to lock it with a satisfying click.

Avery used the next couple of minutes to dust himself down whilst checking from the shadows that his unorthodox arrest had not been witnessed. Satisfied that it had not he consulted his watch once

more and realised he would now have to walk briskly to get back in
time to handover to the nightshift.

Avery changed quickly into his civilian clothes and left the station
whilst the nightshift were still being briefed. If only the criminal
element of the town realised that handovers afforded them the
opportunity to commit crime with minimal risk of apprehension, he
thought as he hurriedly returned to the car park. It had been a risk
leaving the vehicle unattended for the thirty-minute period it had
taken for him to return but thankfully it did not appear to have been
disturbed. A cursory check of the boot showed it to be also as he had
left it with Vickers silent. Perhaps he had suffocated or had just
passed out, Avery thought as drove toward the quarry. He had
chosen the location due to its proximity and restricted access; it was
amongst a long list of 'deposition' locations he had made mental
notes about during solitary nightshift mobile patrols over the
preceding two years. The route was devoid of any cameras and he
had correctly assumed that his colleagues would probably be enjoying
a pre-patrol coffee before venturing out into the cold night.

So, within a relatively short time there he was, leaning up against
the car listening to the now evidently awake and increasingly angry
Mr. Vickers. Avery opened the boot and noted how uncomfortable
Vickers' final journey had been laying on his side in a foetal position.
The burning anger in his eyes was visible in the moonlight as he tried
to communicate some more verbal abuse but was prevented from
doing so by the gag still in place. Avery reached in past the protesting
Vickers and retrieved the green plastic petrol container. As he slowly
unscrewed the top, Vickers' eyes opened ever wider as he struggled
to comprehend his situation. His fears were unlike anything he had
experienced before as the police officer, now not wearing the familiar
uniform that represented order and restraint, began pouring petrol

over him. Avery completed the procedure by opening the car doors and unscrewing the fuel cap, using the remaining fuel to soak the cloth interior of the vehicle. He then returned to the rear of the vehicle and watched the futility of Vickers' efforts to extradite himself from the portable crematorium before taking a few paces back and casually tossing the lit match toward the car. Unlike in the cinema there was so sudden explosion but more of a satisfying 'woof' sound as the car was enveloped in flames. Avery was already walking away; the solitude of the night and his cross-country walk home would provide an hour or so to reflect on how this murder compared to his first all those years ago.

CHAPTER 4

Sebastian Bare was intelligent enough to recognise and understand his own underachievement in life. The disruption of losing his father in a road accident whilst in his mid-teens had been underestimated by those who saw him excel academically before joining the police at the tender age of 19. He had formed a bond with two of his fellow recruits, namely Jim Morton and Paul Avery, with the Instructors at Initial Training School unimaginatively dubbing them 'the three Musketeers'. Any doubts as to Bare's chosen career path were dispelled quickly as he established himself as an officer with exceptional potential. In truth, Bare had been embarrassed at the ease with which he manipulated situations to his advantage. Despite its diversity, basic police work was a straightforward concept to Bare and the accompanying paperwork was an opportunity to subtly improve his practical performance. The results had been dramatic and with minimal real effort in comparison to lumbering colleagues, Bare had, in the space of his two-year probationary period, been transformed from raw recruit to superstar, espoused by peers and bosses alike. Natural progression had taken him into the Criminal Investigation Department where the relaxed supervision further suited his style of police work.

The investment of early unpaid hours and frequent arrests to impress his new bosses paid handsome dividends for young

Detective Constable Bare and his partner, the equally ambitious DC Morton. But, whereas Bare was a natural, Morton certainly was not, frequently hanging onto the shirt-tail of his fellow Musketeer whilst rarely understanding their direction of travel.

Despite their different approaches, there was a great deal of mutual respect between the young detectives. Bare held genuine admiration for the work ethic and attitude of Jim Morton and felt his colleague undersold his worth to the Constabulary. Morton was fiercely determined to progress through the ranks despite his obvious limitations in certain areas. His pairing with the young superstar was an opportunity to bask in some reflected glory but more importantly, for the first time in his career, he had actually begun to enjoy his work. The 'buzz' of making arrests had previously bypassed the rather studious Morton, but Bare's style had somehow stimulated him and the two had become close friends.

After a brief secondment to the tail end of the unsuccessful Vickers murder enquiry their careers both really took off after the McKenzie arrests. Morton had never been a great detective, envying the intuitive senses possessed so evidently by fictional police officers who solved crimes conveniently within the hour episodes on television each evening. He had observed the same trait in a minority of his colleagues, notably Bare, but despite intense scrutiny of his friend's work, Morton knew he would never develop the skill of being a 'natural thief taker'. These were the officers others spoke of in almost reverential terms in the police canteens as exploits were recounted to an appreciative audience of lesser mortals such as Morton.

*

He remembered that day so vividly; he and Bare had been assigned covert observations to combat a growing spate of street muggings within the town centre. They had approached the task with genuine enthusiasm as it represented at that time a rare opportunity to shed the mundanity of reactive investigations and dip their toes into the 'dangerous' world of covert policing.

Morton smiled as he remembered the banter that had accompanied their attempts to assume 'deep cover' by donning baseball caps and sunglasses. Uniformed colleagues dubbed the pair 'Nasty and Crutch' as they left the police station with a swagger that caused the senior sergeant to raise his eyebrows and emit a deep sigh of disapproval. They had hardly moved out of the police building's shadow when Bare suddenly pulled his colleague into a recessed alleyway. Without stopping to explain to his bemused partner, Bare had reached into his breast pocket, switched on his police radio and requested immediate armed assistance.

At first Morton presumed that Bare was role-playing the mocking Starsky and Hutch parts that had been bestowed by their colleagues. The control room response, confirming assistance was en route, quickly changed his mind and he demanded an explanation.

"I think there's a robbery going on at that Building Society," said Bare, making a minimal nod in the direction of the building on the opposite side of the road.

Morton's incredulous expression turned into one of shock as an ear-piercing audible alarm suddenly came from the direction of the identified premises.

"Fuck," was Bare's only response before running across the road toward the building.

Morton instinctively followed without knowing what was happening or what Bare intended to do. The sudden emergence from the Building Society of two individuals wearing crash helmets and carrying rucksacks clarified the situation somewhat although Morton, in truth, found it difficult to observe anything other than the sawn-off shotguns the robbers were also carrying. Bare was already several yards ahead and showed no signs of slowing down as he reached the opposite pavement, crashing into the escaping pair like a bull exacting retribution on a pair of rodeo clowns. Bare's momentum in fact took himself and one of the robbers back into the doorway of the Building Society, their journey abruptly ending as a mesh security grille belatedly dropped over the door. The second offender's attempt to scramble to his feet was prevented by the rugby tackle instinctively employed by the arriving Morton. Within seconds, although it had seemed like hours, the four fighting men were joined by a cacophony of sirens as police officers appeared from all directions. Morton grimly held onto his prey until he was prised away by an armed officer who was bellowing incomprehensible instructions in his right ear. Bare, in contrast, had virtually thrown his prisoner at the first of the arriving officers and had used his free hands to recover his police radio which had spilled onto the ground during the struggle. Having recovered the equipment Bare wasted no time in transmitting details of a red Ford Sierra that he believed had been the intended get-away car, which had sped away moments earlier.

In the sanctuary of the police bar an hour later, Bare told a still bemused Morton how the heroes had foiled an armed robbery.

"I saw that Sierra drive past us, three up, as we were walking up Drayton Road. The passengers were wearing those bloody stupid blue overalls. Then as we were opposite the Building Society, I saw two guys wearing what looked like the same overalls walk in, only this time they had crash helmets on. The Sierra was parked in the lay-by further up the road," said Bare, adding the additional detail concerning the vehicle as he was mentally recalling the scene.

"I never saw any of that," Morton had replied, full of self-recrimination.

"Well it's a good job you reacted so quickly," said Bare with genuine appreciation. "We would have been fucked if they had realised what was happening."

Morton concurred and wondered how long it would take before he could pick up his pint glass without it shaking violently. They were joined by Paul Avery who was the latest in a long line of congratulatory officers. Whilst most had sought each salacious detail from the dynamic duo, Avery in contrast merely placed two glasses of scotch on the table in front of them.

"Well then you stupid bastards, I guess you are off Stuart McKenzie's Christmas card list."

Avery's reference to the infamous head of the McKenzie crime family caused Morton to hurriedly gulp the recently presented scotch as he was caused to consider the potential ramifications of arresting the crime lord's sons for armed robbery.

Bare, by contrast slowly savoured the drink and replied, "What happened to all for one and one for all?"

"Ah, would love to help but my transfer to the Met has just come through," announced the soon to be departing third Musketeer.

It was the last time the three would share a drink for many years. Avery needed the anonymity of a Metropolitan Force, Morton would quietly progress through the ranks and Bare, despite being promoted first would remain at the rank of Sergeant.

As a consequence of his promotion Bare returned to uniform duties with conspicuously shiny stripes affixed to his sleeves. The initial thrill of his new-found status quickly subsided as he watched with envy as his former colleagues in CID moved from one major investigation to another. It would be surely too simplistic to cite boredom as the catalyst for what happened next, but after years of self-reflection, Bare had yet to come up with a more plausible theory to explain that time. In simple terms, Sergeant Bare simply and inexplicably stopped driving forward. Although he still saw the opportunities he became ambivalent about taking them. Previously welcome distractions like women and gambling suddenly became the driving forces in his life. He began to resent his time at work because it intruded into the space he increasingly needed for visits to the racecourse or to chase some skirt that lost his interest as soon as it capitulated to his fraudulent charm. He was still held in high regard by his colleagues and did just enough to maintain that standing but, if anyone had bothered to look, they would have seen that he was treading water, long before he was entitled to do so. His friendship with Morton was there in name only and they both used the excuse of different work patterns to gradually slow down and eventually stop their socialising together. Morton's work ethic ensured that steady progression and a two-year secondment to the Home Office further distanced the colleagues both in a literal and ideological sense. The antidote for Bare's career paralysis was named Julia Addison.

CHAPTER 5

She had lied at her interview. There had been no childhood aspiration to follow in her late father's footsteps and serve the local community. There was no driving ambition to right wrongs and bring criminals to justice. Julia didn't even consider the healthcare package to be particularly attractive but felt it prudent to cite it to the attentive Chief Constable and the other two members of the interview panel. Whilst telling the truth was certainly what an aspiring police officer ought to have done, even the most naïve postgraduate would surely have done the same and told them what they were clearly so keen to hear. The chosen mode of dress for the interview had been equally calculated, a seemingly respectable two-piece grey suit with a skirt that revealed just a little too much leg, which was to the Chief Officers' barely disguised delight, when she sat down before them.

Even at the relatively young age of twenty-two, Julia Addison found it easy to manipulate older men and was amazed that her peers didn't appear to have worked out the benefits that could be accrued by following suit. It wasn't particularly hard to identify that men needed their egos massaged and Julia had a variety of techniques to do just that. Her undoubted favourite was the subtle combination of innocence, sexuality and a seemingly endless capacity to hang on a man's every word as though he were a wise prophet sent to enlighten the female species. To this end, she was aided by her shoulder-length blonde hair, bright blue eyes and sparkling smile. She had an athletic figure rather than the curvier one she would have preferred but her long slender legs more than made up for anything else. Judging by the Chief Constable's gaze, he would have concurred with that view. She knew that she was becoming increasingly cynical but, 'hey, there was nobody else left now who would look out for her.'

She snapped out of her brief and unexpected psychoanalysis just in time to hear the tail end of the Chief's speech about his vision of policing. Julia met the conclusion with her sweetest smile and knew that it was in the bag. As night followed day, she would soon be WPC Addison on a nice annual salary and living in comfortable surroundings. It would do until something or someone better came along and despite herself, she may even have some fun along the way.

The months that followed were generally happy ones. Police Training School had been less academically challenging than University and the physical side had provided another opportunity to excel for the athletic new officer. She regretted the fling with the married drill sergeant but only after it became general knowledge toward the end of her training period. Luckily his reputation preceded him and she was happy to play the wide-eyed, impressionable student role that others cast her in. Despite this, she had still faced a stern rebuke from the training Inspector who had been a former colleague of her father. The rebuke lost all impact as she revealed that it was the anniversary of the tragic car accident that had seen the death of both her parents. The Inspector reddened at his own insensitivity. Julia smiled inwardly and added a tragic past to her armoury of weapons of mass manipulation.

Whilst her arrival at her first posting had been impactive for her new male colleagues and especially Sergeant Bare, Julia had considered it a disappointing start to her new career. Her assigned station was in the less salubrious part of the county and the building itself reflected that. From the outside it had reminded her of a concrete fort perched at the top of a small hill, overlooking the little grey town below. The décor inside had done little to lift her spirits with tired furniture crammed into offices discoloured by years of cigarette smoke. The personnel at the station comprised of a mixture of young, fresh-faced officers experiencing their first taste of policing and battle-hardened veterans who knew to the day how long was left of their thirty years' service. The canteen cook who had seemingly been in post since the inception of policing, referred to the officers as her 'boys and girls' and although everybody moaned about everything it all seemed to tick along with the rhythm of a large dysfunctional family.

A significant part of the wall in the Briefing Room was taken up with a hierarchal chart listing all personnel currently assigned to the Station, those of Sergeant Rank and above had a photograph next to their name. Each Sergeant was in charge of a team of officers whose names were listed below their supervisory officer. Julia wondered what determined the order of the listing as it was clearly not done alphabetically or chronologically based on the officer's unique epaulette number. What was apparent though was that none of the ranking officers were female and that the 'WPC' assigned to each section was listed last in the list. Her father, unusually for his generation and gender, had been a staunch feminist and would not have allowed such an overt display of sexism in his building. But as well as promoting those values he had also been a master in the art of implementing change in an almost invisible way. She recalled his favourite phrase that he had urged her to recite and learn as a life lesson, *"Diplomacy is the art of telling somebody to go to hell in such a way that they look forward to the trip."*

The Inspector walked into the Briefing Room and proffered no apology for his late arrival. Julia smiled a greeting but waited until eye contact had been established after the obligatory tits and leg check before she greeted him with a, "Morning, sir."

'Morning, young lady, welcome to the Bronx." He smiled at his own 'humorous' remark and she took the cue to smile back. "You will be on Sergeant Bare's team so you will be in good hands. We will catch up for a proper chat once you settle in."

"Look forward to that, sir," replied Julia confidently, masking her distain but with a self-assurance that seemed to disarm her senior officer.

'Err, good, right, must go, have a wander around, get to know the place." And then as an afterthought he said, "Knew your dad, good copper," but by then he was already striding away before she could agree.

Her next appointment with her new Sergeant was still an hour away so she took the Inspector's advice and 'had a wander' culminating in the large oak-panelled room on the top floor with its imposing door sign stating "Major Incident Room – Authorised Personnel Only". She felt confident that the absence of anyone in the room and its scant occupancy of piled desks and chairs meant the sign only applied when the room was in use for its reserved purpose.

It was the same room that would host the team investigating the death of Julia Bare, née Addison, some twenty-three years later.

CHAPTER 6

The first three years of their relationship was like a flame, fed with oxygen, making it burn with intensity admired by all others around. The spark was there from that first introductory handshake and Sergeant Bare knew that his new team member was unlike any of her colleagues. The physical attraction was obvious but the electricity of her touch was something different and her eyes held him in a seemingly unbreakable hypnotic trance. He was smitten and wrongfooted as the patter that normally flowed had somehow got lost between his brain and mouth. In fact he found himself talking like a model supervisory officer performing a welcoming routine in the same manner as the cabin crew would on an aircraft. Lots of smiles and little substance.

Julia experienced similar feelings as the sight of this tall, good-looking man in Sergeant's uniform, a most welcome addition to the dismal surroundings she was slowly coming to terms with. She felt herself blushing for no good reason and was both embarrassed and surprised by this physiological reaction. Any third-party onlooker who knew both of them would have been amused by the rapidly unfolding relationship but there was no such person and the backdrop of a busy police station camouflaged the scene.

"Welcome to the real world," said Bare, slowly regaining his composure as he gave the guided tour of the station in all its urban glory. He took the opportunity to lightly place an unnecessary guiding hand on Julia's arm as they walked through into the custody area. A 55-year-old tramp called Jack was sitting patiently on a small wooden bench bolted to the tiled custody complex floor. Jack's odour was in stark contrast to the sterile smell of the room that had seen thousands of people stand before the imposing reception area over the years. Petty thieves, increasingly with a drug dependency, Saturday night fighters and juveniles were the standard customers. Rarely, a celebrity criminal or murderer would grace the station with their presence but the reception routine would take little account of their status, treating each one with a tried and tested monotony – search, rights and cell.

To the outside world and even to the intrusive police family, Sergeant and Constable had purely a professional arrangement. In their private world, however, the two had become lovers within weeks. Fate had accelerated the process as they found to their mutual amazement that Julia's decision to purchase a modest flat in the town had made them virtually neighbours, separated only by a small communal parking area.

Sebastian was surprised that he was capable of feeling such emotion for any woman but he proved to be a surprisingly considerate and caring lover, capable of gestures of genuine tenderness. These were traits that few of his previous conquests would have recognised. The majority of his previous associations had been a combination of opportunity and convenience with little necessity and even less desire for any degree of commitment, faked or not. At some point, having sex had turned into making love. He found Julia to be remarkably athletic and adventurous, with a seemingly bottomless pit of new ideas with which to surprise him and a near insatiable appetite.

It had been a mutual decision to keep their relationship a closely guarded secret which somehow added to the excitement. On a more practical level, neither wanted a change in their working lives that a public declaration would have surely caused. The police service was decidedly uncomfortable about couples working together especially when one held a supervisory role. The lengths they went to were elaborate enough never to raise a flicker of suspicion in colleagues' minds.

Both quickly discovered the downside of not being publicly attached was that they were not immune from rumour and gossip about their respective partner. Julia, therefore, quickly learned of Bare's predatory past from a succession of spurned exes who each decided to confide in her. She suspected that the given reason for warning about the intentions of her Sergeant masked the actual fact that the majority of his conquests had revelled in their previous encounter. Bare quickly learned of WPC Addison's training school exploits as her conquest there had once been a good friend of his. Both recognised their pasts as being something of a 'spent conviction' and suppressed any desire to discuss it in front of the other. After all, the present was what was important and the present was pretty good at the moment.

Before they had met, Julia had never wanted more than sexual fulfilment and a social life from a relationship and for Bare it had been just the sex. It was therefore a surprise to both of them when they started planning the possibility of living together and selling Julia's flat within six months of her purchase of it. Of course, it was only a matter of time before the relationship was 'outed' despite their sustained secrecy. Bizarrely, they were spotted by a station clerk whilst enjoying a romantic weekend break in Belgium. The clerk had travelled to Brussels as part of his never-ending quest to record train numbers in a cherished notebook but instead his study of a quiet platform revealed a couple of his work colleagues enjoying a rare public show of affection, walking hand in hand towards him. Bare recovered from the initial shock of seeing the clerk and immediately dropped to one knee and proposed to a truly bewildered Julia. It was an incredibly spontaneous gesture that was recounted at length by the clerk who returned to work two days earlier than the newly engaged couple.

Predictably their public-facing liberal employer turned inwardly into a Victorian father affronted by the moral outrage of such decadent behaviour within the ranks and sought to separate the pair at least professionally. But Bare, already anticipating this response had already applied for a Detective Sergeant's position at another station thereby solving the problem he had created.

The wedding had been a modest one attended by only a few close friends and even fewer relatives. Jim Morton had performed the role of Best Man with outstanding preparation and attention to detail. His speech had been heralded as a masterclass which was gratifying as it had cost an expensive bottle of wine when purchasing it from a colleague much more adept at the creation of such things. Bare of course had surmised he was listening to a third party's wit and wisdom but it made him even more grateful for the efforts Morton had made. Because he knew his friend so well he was also the only person to spot the Best Man's hesitancy midway through reading aloud the pile of cards from absent well-wishers.

After the speeches, obligatory toasts and cake cutting, Bare sought out his friend and proffered a congratulatory handshake.

"Can I see it, Jim?" he asked.

"See what?" replied the reddening Morton; subterfuge had never been his strong point.

Bare merely raised his eyebrows and Morton reluctantly retrieved the card from his jacket pocket where he thought he had skilfully secreted it mid-speech.

At first glance the card appeared indistinguishable from the many others that had been passed to Morton prior to his speech. White flowers adorned the front but inside the printed greeting offered condolences as opposed to congratulations. Underneath the printed words someone had added their own personalised message in neat handwriting:

"Now that you have a family you will understand what it's like to experience real pain and loss."

The annotation was unsigned but Bare's opinion based on nothing more than intuition was that it had been penned by a female.

"Well I can understand why you skipped that one, would have dropped the mood a bit," said Bare with a nonchalant smile.

"What do you want me to do with it?" replied Morton with some relief that his unexpected burden had now been shared.

Bare shrugged. "Just chuck it, Jim, we have both had worse, it's nothing."

"But it could be construed as a threat," said Morton in a hushed, almost conspiratorial tone. "It might be a message from Scotland," he added with the unnecessary less than cryptic clue.

"No, it's not their style to send nice greeting cards, more likely to be one of the ones who I didn't marry, just bin it."

'Okay, if you are sure," said a partly reassured Morton.

"Cheers Jim, now I need to go find my wife," said a departing Bare, leaving his friend with a friendly arm pat.

En route to his new bride Bare took a full glass from a passing waitress's tray and gulped the contents in one swig. That was the third message he had received that week.

CHAPTER 7

The Present

The two McKenzie brothers had each received a substantial custodial sentence for the robbery. Any chance of an early release had evaporated when the two had received a further sentence for taking turns to beat a fellow inmate with a pool cue during their communal recreation period. Only the timely intervention of several prison officers had ensured the additional charge sheet cited GBH as opposed to murder. Unlike his sons, Stuart Mackenzie did not blame the incarceration of his heirs on those young detectives although he was annoyed with the level of accolades the local media had bestowed on them. The elder brother, Liam, had sought his father's permission to commit the crime as was the hierarchal system in the crime family. Liam's perpetual eagerness had been accelerated by the news his wife was pregnant and he had been anxious to fund a better lifestyle. Stuart had reviewed the proposal and had concluded it had been hastily conceived. He had told his son to do more work to eliminate obvious risks and had struggled to hide his displeasure that such a rudimentary 'business plan' had been placed before him. Whilst not exactly of 'mafioso' standing he wanted his Organised Crime Group to be perceived as committing crime with a certain sophistication and an 'across the pavement' robbery didn't fall into that category.

Class A drug supply was still more lucrative to the family and continual management and oversight of an increasing network had ensured risks were mitigated. But just as the end users of their product needed to feed their addiction so Liam needed the adrenaline rush of dynamic criminality. He had cajoled his younger brother Sean into joining him and together with a trusted cousin whose nickname 'Wheels' accurately described his supporting role, the three set off. Liam had promised his wife Shannon that the shotguns would not be loaded and were for show only. He was true to his word mainly because of his supreme confidence that his manner alone would cause meek bank employees to capitulate.

Their modest haul amounted to less than £8,000 as cash tills were hurriedly emptied by petrified staff. Nevertheless, Liam had found the experience exhilarating as he exited the building focusing only on the nearby waiting escape vehicle. The unexpected impact of a 14-stone man into his midriff therefore took his breath away both in surprise and literally. A few minutes later as he lay face-down on the cold pavement, handcuffed behind his back, he visualised that familiar expression of disappointment on his father's face.

Now separated from his younger sibling, Liam was in familiar pose stretched out on his bed staring at the ceiling of his single-occupied prison cell. He was aware of the prison officer's presence and had obviously heard his name being called. He had chosen to ignore it as one of the many 'power-play' interactions he enjoyed with any form of authority figure on a daily basis. Finally after recording yet another 'win' in his own mind he elected to acknowledge the officer's presence.

"You have a visitor, McKenzie, follow me," said the prison officer.

McKenzie took a moment to digest the information; unplanned

visits normally fell into one of two categories, legal or personal. If it were the former it would most likely be some cops on a fishing expedition, the latter would be worse, however, as those visits tended to be on compassionate grounds.

'Who is it?" McKenzie asked in as casual a tone as possible as he slowly rose to his feet.

The prison officer checked the visitor log on the clipboard he was carrying. "Says Mrs McKenzie," he stated as he turned to escort the prisoner to the visitors' interview area.

Although concerned as to the news she might be delivering McKenzie walked enthusiastically alongside his escort. He had not seen Shannon for several weeks, suspecting she had been using a succession of excuses to avoid the two-hour journey to the prison. Whatever the reason for the visit he would ensure he used the opportunity to tell her face to face it wasn't acceptable and she should be bringing his young son as well. 'Daddy working away' just didn't cut it anymore. By the time he arrived at the modern purpose-built visitors' centre with its impersonal, CCTV-covered interview booths, McKenzie was spoiling for an argument. His rising temper soon dissipated though as he entered his allotted booth and saw it was his mother patiently waiting for him on the other side of the reinforced glass partition.

Despite every one of Mary McKenzie's male relatives having served time at Her Majesty's pleasure at some stage of their lives this was her first ever visit to such an establishment. It had been as grim as she had anticipated and the indignity of the search procedures conducted at the entrance made her silently vow never to return whatever the circumstances. Even the first sight of her eldest son in a number of years did little to appease the sudden onset of claustrophobia she was experiencing.

"What's up, Ma?" greeted Liam, conditioned by years of incarceration not to display any overt concern.

"Your dad is dying, son." She wasted no time in delivering her news or attempting to soften the blow with any words of comfort.

Liam listened in silence as his mother expanded on her opening statement. He didn't really take in all the detail, something about a cancer diagnosis over a year ago, that wider dissemination of it had been forbidden by his father for fear of showing weakness to his rivals. Something about a recent move into a hospital. No, wait, a hospice, whatever the fuck that was. And oh yes, even if he secured early release next year it would be too late to see his dad again, way too late.

As Mary broke the news she saw things only a mother would see, the tiniest of movements of his top lip when for the briefest of time he became her 8-year-old vulnerable son as opposed to the hardened criminal sitting in sullen silence. She spoke of other things, Shannon, his son and even something about her proposed journey home but he had stopped listening. He could never recall his father saying that he was proud of him let alone anything about love, but his adoration of Stuart McKenzie, the indestructible larger-than-life Glaswegian was absolute. If his 'da' had voluntarily gone into a hospice as it sounded, then he had already given up, something the big man would never do. His dad was already dead, he concluded.

His mother cut short their meeting, ensuring she had exactly half her allotted visiting time to deliver the same agony message to her younger son. Sean was a more sensitive soul so she adopted a much softer approach, bracing herself for the inevitable anguished cries that seemed to echo around the whole complex. She had implored the staff to keep a special eye on Sean as she was genuinely fearful as to how he would cope with continued imprisonment when all he wanted to do was be with his beloved 'da' in his final days. The staff assured her they would but when she searched their eyes for genuine compassion none was to be found so she doubted their word.

During her journey home she replayed in her mind the last conversation she had with Stuart at his bedside the night before. She didn't know whether it had been a side effect of the morphine flowing through his body or a desire to unburden himself of the secret he had been carrying, maybe a combination of the two. Either way she wished he had taken it to his grave rather than transfer the burden of knowledge onto her shoulders. She wouldn't visit him again as her anger outweighed the grief of losing her husband of forty years. No wonder he had always told his family to never trust the police.

CHAPTER 8

"That jockey couldn't ride a fucking rocking horse."

It was meant to be a thought, at worst a muttered utterance. Instead the magnitude of the disappointment was replicated by the volume of the exclamation, causing disapproving looks from fellow guests in the corporate hospitality marquee. Bare continued to stare at the large TV screen, unrepentant despite his wife hissing, "Sebastian, will you remember where you are?" Bare needed no reminder regarding his whereabouts, in a fucking tent at a racecourse surrounded by bloody chattering idiots who didn't know one end of a horse from the other. Whereas he, the expert, had just backed four successive losers and was two hundred down on the day.

His spirits were not exactly lifted as he observed his boss, Detective Inspector Jim Morton, walk toward him, hand in hand with the very desirable Stephanie. By contrast, Morton was having a good day. His wife appeared genuinely attentive to him despite other demands associated with being responsible for the corporate guests. He was enjoying a rare day away from his desk and much to his surprise had received £200 winnings from a randomly placed bet on the last race.

It was a rare social outing for the pair of couples, albeit Stephanie was there in an official capacity as the event organiser. Bare had politely declined other invitations in the past but the opportunity to access a free bar whilst witnessing his favourite sport had seemed a good idea at the time.

"How's your luck, Bare?" enquired Morton, the use of his Detective Sergeant's last name reflecting Sebastian Bare's desire for his first name to be restricted wherever possible.

"Up and down, Jim," lied Bare. "Have you had a bet, Steph?"

"Gambling is all a bit of a mystery to me," replied Mrs Morton, enjoying the way her husband's Sergeant was looking at her. She was immaculate as always, the designer outfit accentuating her natural assets and her wide-brimmed hat, worn at exactly the right angle, adding its own statement.

The three became four as Julia Bare joined them positively gushing about the splendour of the occasion and the surroundings. By contrast, she was more comfortably attired, unsure of the dress code for such an occasion in the Members' Enclosure. Her husband had been of little help to her, merely assuring her that she looked fine, and swiftly adding that they were in danger of missing the first race.

Bare used the offer of a drink to accompany Morton to the bar.

"Julia seems to be enjoying herself," Morton remarked after ordering a round of champagne despite Bare's preference for a large vodka.

The junior officer ignored the subtle reference to his wife's growing alcohol intake and studied his race card in preparation for the next race. The potential winner, identified whilst studying the form in his newspaper that morning, now seemed no more likely than any of the other seven runners. This was a common phenomenon when successive losses affect your confidence, he reassured himself.

"What are you doing in the next race, Jim?" Bare heard himself ask.

Morton, eager as ever to assist, frowned as he studied the list of runners and riders. He was a self-professed novice at the Sport of Kings although remarkably was in profit to the tune of £354 on the day. The jumbled array of figures that appeared to be randomly placed around each listed horse meant nothing to him, so he concentrated on the names instead.

"How about 'King Stuart' in honour of the late Stuart McKenzie?" offered Morton.

Bare bristled; his intended bet had indeed been "King Stuart" but the newly established link to his nemesis caused him to re-select.

"I can't believe that man went to his grave without ever seeing the inside of a prison cell," he said, making no attempt to hide the bitterness he felt.

"Well perhaps without him in charge we can dismantle the whole network?" offered Morton.

"Yeah, perhaps," said Bare as he pencil circled his new selection with the confidence of a condemned man walking toward the execution chamber.

Having placed his bet on the rails with a trackside bookmaker, Bare hastened to return to watch the race on the large screen TV within the marquee. He would have preferred to remain outside but etiquette dictated he return to his hosts. Predictably, his re-selection was pipped at the post by the grey "King Stuart". The deafening cheer suggested that the majority around him had decided that Morton was on a hot streak and worthy of following. A rare sparkle in his wife's eyes suggested that she too had been lucky and her happiness surprisingly eased his growing discontent.

He was joined again by Morton who was unable to suppress the joy of another payout much to the growing irritation of Bare. Perhaps sensing his friend wasn't going to be receptive to another tip Morton changed the subject of their conversation, predictably slipping back into work mode.

"Have you heard who is favourite for Head of Crime?"

Bare had not heard and didn't particularly care. He expected the vacant position would be filled by some clone of the departed incumbent as that was the way the senior officer carousel seemed to work. As long as they remained on the top floor and didn't scrutinise his overtime or claim forms too much he had no preference as to their identity.

Morton leaned closer eager to share the juicy gossip he had overheard.

"Paul Avery," he said in hushed tones.

"Blimey," replied Bare, genuinely surprised at the revelation. He had not really kept track of Avery's career since he had left but had always assumed their paths would follow a similar route, now it appeared Avery had gained a three-rank lead over his one-time friend. "You two in the same Lodge, Jim?"

Morton ignored the masonic jibe; his membership of that much maligned organisation had actually been something of an anti-climax despite assurances from his late father-in-law that it would yield enormous professional benefit. At least he would no longer have to deal with Worshipful Brother McKenzie, he thought with some consolation, perhaps his luck was finally turning for the better. His rare optimistic mood barely lasted an hour. After receiving a call from the withheld number and listening with growing resignation to the female voice calling to introduce herself, he silently replaced the phone in his jacket pocket. He had been naive to think that Stuart McKenzie would keep his word.

CHAPTER 9

Soon-to-be Detective Superintendent Avery had one last job to undertake in London. He could of course have let it go but suspected it would have remained an unscratched itch and life was too short for such irritations.

He had attended the lecture alongside his senior colleagues with genuine interest. The Metropolitan Police were very good at enabling continuous professional development of their staff, something he would take back with him when he assumed command in his home town. In fact it was beyond interest, the lecture entitled 'Serial Killers, who they are and how to recognise them' was something he was desperate to experience. Of course as he and his colleagues waited for Professor Stimpson to arrive he had bemoaned the inconvenience of being away from his desk for such an unnecessary input. "Serial killers are not really an everyday problem," he had asserted to those in his immediate proximity. "Cybercrime is what we need training in," he added as a further justification of his view.

Professor Stimpson was an annoyingly erudite speaker, inflaming Avery's discontent further as he saw the appreciative and attentive looks on his colleagues' faces within minutes of the lecture starting.

"Of course the lecture title is a misnomer," Stimpson proclaimed. "Unfortunately I can't supply all of you with a generic profile of an average serial killer but I am able to give you a concise summary of years of research into the subject. Firstly let me dispel a few myths. Real-life serial killers are not the isolated monsters of fiction, the majority are not reclusive social misfits and very often they are able to successfully hide in plain sight. Yes, ladies and gentlemen, they walk amongst us."

Professor Stimpson had delivered the same lecture many times worldwide and paused momentarily for the appreciative chuckle from his audience that invariably followed his opening rhetoric.

"Those who successfully blend in are typically also employed, have families, own homes and outwardly appear to be normal members of society. There is often a pattern of them being overlooked by law enforcement officials as well as their own families and peers because all our instincts are to seek out the unusual rather than the innocuous," continued the renowned criminologist.

Avery was disappointed that the lecture appeared to be following a tired format. One superficial observation followed another as he scanned the audience for a kindred spirit. Instead he was met by a sea of attentive faces apparently hanging on Stimpson's every word. *If he talks about the MacDonald Triad I will scream,* thought Avery.

"Which brings me onto the MacDonald Triad," announced Stimpson mid-lecture. "Basically research has indicated there are three signs that can indicate whether someone will grow up to be a serial killer or at least a violent offender. The classic behaviours are being cruel to animals, committing minor acts of arson and enuresis," said the Professor before pausing and waiting for the inevitable question from at least one of the Detectives in the room.

"Sorry, Professor, what is enuresis?" asked a voice from someone diligently taking notes in the front row.

"It means bedwetting," announced Avery before Stimpson could respond much to the hilarity of Scotland Yard's finest.

He restrained from further interjection as the lecture rumbled on, somewhat disillusioned that the eminent academic was still trotting out research published in 1963. He had been tempted to ask a question or two at the end of the session but any further emergence from the anonymity of the crowd might have caused unnecessary attention, he reasoned. The Professor's answer to the question about whether psychopaths tended to be more intelligent than average did, however, intrigue him.

"Psychopathy is a personality disorder manifested in people who use a mixture of charm, manipulation, intimidation, and occasionally violence to control others, in order to satisfy their own selfish needs. There is no correlation between this condition and intelligence; my personal opinion is that a psychopath would often assume he was more intelligent but this is just delusional on his part," Stimpson concluded.

Avery wondered why the Professor had provided a single personal opinion right at the end of a lecture that had not been based on scientific research. He hoped it was as a result of the high-profile case a few years earlier when Stimpson had barely survived a withering cross examination by a defendant conducting his own defence. Whilst a conviction had followed mainly in spite of the professor's testimony the reputational damage suffered had caused the loss of a lucrative position at the FBI Academy and forced him back onto the lecture circuit.

After waiting for the room to clear Avery slowly crossed to the lectern where Stimpson was busy putting away his notes.

"Fascinating stuff, Professor," he gushed, offering an outstretched hand.

"Thank you, I hope it was of some interest," replied Stimpson, his standard response to such greetings.

"Oh, it was brilliant," enthused Avery. "I have read a lot of your publications and wondered if I could pick your brains about a case I am working on?"

"Well there is a procedure to go through if you want my professional opinion," Stimpson began to explain but stopped short as he realised the good-looking younger man was still holding his hand.

"I was hoping for more of a personal meeting?" said Avery. "Something more intimate over a drink perhaps?" he added with unnecessary clarity.

It had been a while since Stimpson had been so blatantly propositioned; normally his encounters with young attractive men had to be paid for these days. He felt himself blush as he told Avery the name of the hotel he was staying at. The addition of his room number reaffirming how intimate he hoped their meeting that evening would be.

As Avery returned to his office he wondered if someone of average intelligence could ascertain someone's sexuality so quickly and then masquerade as a suitor with such authenticity. He doubted it and allowed himself a moment of smugness before settling down to formulate his plan.

CHAPTER 10

Mary McKenzie slowly sipped her glass of red wine as she opened and read the stack of cards on the table before her. She barely recognised the man described in such glowing terms by those who offered such heartfelt sympathy for his loss. The disproportionately large dining room was silent save for the repetitive tick of the ornate clock on the sideboard. The clock had been a present from her husband some years earlier and she hated it as much now as she had done when he had enthusiastically presented it to her years earlier. She realised now it personified him perfectly, an ostentatious display of wealth but with no class.

The family would need to be redefined, she had decided; whilst it made perfect sense for his brothers to be involved, especially in the absence of her sons, there were too many cousins and nephews that Stuart had taken under his wing without consulting her. The business was lucrative but didn't feel as secure as it had been before although she was supremely confident no one would dare to challenge her position of overall control. Stuart had effectively paved the way for years by proclaiming her to be the real brains of the outfit. She had been content to play the role of supportive wife confident in the knowledge he would consult her before making major decisions. Well that was until his dying declaration of course, that had shocked her to the core. Now that her anger had dissipated she had begun to understand his decision but she doubted she would ever forgive him even posthumously.

Her train of thought was interrupted as she heard the front door open and the familiar excited footsteps running toward her. The boy entered the room with his arms already stretched wide in anticipation of a welcoming hug from his beloved grandmother.

"Grandma, Grandma!" shouted the excited 8-year-old boy as he flung his arms around Mary as she rose to greet him.

The boy's mother, Shannon, followed her son at a more sedate pace, weighed down by the recently acquired purchases made during their shopping expedition.

"We bought you a present because you are still sad about Grandad," enthused Cameron in an excited tone that suggested his own transient period of grief had ended. His grandfather, in marked contrast to Mary had been somewhat of a remote and cold figure in his life so whilst he had cried upon hearing the news of his death Cameron had moved onto other things quite quickly. His main sadness at the funeral had been observing his grandmother's tears that had only abated when he had instinctively held her hand as an act of comfort. He had received a look of approval from his dad who was unable to provide the same comfort due to being handcuffed to the accompanying prison guard.

"Oh my, how exciting," said Mary who had still yet to acknowledge her daughter-in-law's presence in the room.

"Cameron chose it himself," interjected Shannon, "didn't you, babe?"

Mary struggled to contain her annoyance at the term of endearment contained within Shannon's rhetorical question.

"You're not a babe anymore, are you Cameron?" she retorted, eliciting the support of her grandson with a well-timed wink.

"No, I'm not. Stop calling me that, Mum," said the instantly indignant boy.

After the presentation of a hand-painted and recently glazed plate proclaiming 'Grandma rocks' had been completed, together with accompanying detail of how skilfully Cameron had composed the piece, he and his mother left the room to put away the rest of the shopping. They had occupied the adjoining ground-floor annexe of the large house since Liam McKenzie had been incarcerated. It had been Stuart's suggestion, no, command, to keep his family safe and united. The collateral benefit for Mary was that she got to see her grandson every day and although she had never vocalised it she was concerned what would happen upon Liam's release.

Shannon too was concerned about her husband's release and wondered if it would lead to a resumption of the domestic violence she had regularly suffered at his hand pre-sentence. She had found it difficult to judge whether prison had changed Liam but the flashes of anger so evident in his eyes when she infrequently visited him suggested not. She drew comfort from the fact that Mary had wholeheartedly supported her decision not to take Cameron to that horrible place although the pretence of his dad's whereabouts had long since been removed. Liam might have used the lack of parental contact with his son to justify a physical reaction but he would never adopt a contrary stance to his mother who he both loved and feared in equal measure.

Mary held the newly acquired plate before her and smiled as she noted the additional detail of a tiny St Andrew's flag underneath where Cameron had proudly signed it. She was pleased to note that also in the presentation box that it had arrived in was a small wooden display stand. She walked over to the sideboard, picked up the clock and without hesitation strode outside and dropped into the black bin designed for household rubbish. Disappointingly a full bin bag deposited in there earlier cushioned the fall and the clock face stared back at her defiantly. Not content, she retrieved the object d'art before ceremoniously dropping it from head height onto the stone driveway. The clock landed with a satisfying smash meaning that it took her a while to bend down and carefully place the broken fragments back into the bin. Job done, she returned to the dining room and ensured her new centrepiece was carefully positioned in place of the clock.

CHAPTER 11

The evening had started so well. *How the hell have I ended up here?* was the recurring thought of Professor Stimpson as he balanced precariously on the chair desperately hoping the belt around his neck wouldn't tighten any further.

Three hours earlier he had emerged from the shower and contemplated whether to dress or just wear the white hotel-supplied towelling robe. When the handsome detective arrived he could apologise profusely that he hadn't time to dress with the obvious hope the younger man would not be at all disappointed. With that script in mind he checked himself in the brightly illuminated bathroom mirror and applied a modest amount of expensive aftershave. He had never been a handsome man in the classical sense, shorter than average and with a receding hairline from an early age, being the two main areas of his discontent. As he had got older bad eating habits had caught up with him and he was now much heavier than he had ever been. For a moment he allowed the creeping doubt to re-enter his mind that no attractive younger man could possibly be interested in him. He contemplated cancelling the 'date' if indeed that's what it was but then realised he had no means of communicating with the man, such had been the brevity of their earlier encounter at the conclusion of his lecture. He wasn't even sure of the guy's name, *But there again why does that matter?* he thought as he flashed his nice smile into the mirror, vowing to savour the unexpected company.

Avery arrived promptly at the hotel and was already familiar with its layout having studied numerous photographs that had accompanied glowing online reviews. Travelling lecturers obviously charge a premium rate, he correctly assumed after noting the exorbitant room rates even by London standards. Concerned about CCTV he used the extravagant bouquet of flowers to mask his face as he safely negotiated the busy lobby without challenge. He elected to take the stairs rather than the lift and was delighted to see there appeared to be no camera coverage of that area. Within moments he was at the door where Stimpson eagerly responded to his light knock.

As well as the flowers Avery was holding a supermarket carrier bag in his gloved hands and after presenting the bouquet he produced a bottle of very expensive vodka from it. Stimpson would have preferred wine but masked any disappointment with gushing gratitude and then an apology that they would have to make use of the glasses supplied by the hotel for bathroom use. Stimpson presumed that the remaining contents of the bag were merely the residue of Avery's personal shopping as it was left on the floor as they both sat on the sofa conspicuously close to the ornate king-sized bed. Avery remarked how beautiful the room was, with its many original features, he seemed to be both surprised and delighted to note the suspended dark oak beams that ran across the width of the room.

As the two sat talking and drinking, Stimpson's doubts began to resurface. The conversation had almost entirely centred on his work and research despite his attempts to engage Avery with increasingly tactile responses. He had even allowed his robe to 'accidentally' fall open at one point but to his immense disappointment the younger man took no apparent notice. Just as he was resigning himself to the fact he had horribly misread the situation Avery suddenly and unexpectedly suggested they watch some porn together.

Stimpson wasted no time in setting up his laptop, although his vodka consumption somewhat slowed his thought processes. He could sense Avery's demeanour had changed; the previously friendly tone in his voice was now much more curt and authoritative. Stimpson became aroused by this new masterful side to his companion's persona.

"I have a particular fetish," confided Avery as began watching some of Stimpson's favourite collection of erotic cinema.

"Do you now?" said Stimpson, puzzled that his increasing strokes of Avery's thigh were producing no obvious physical reaction.

"Autoerotic asphyxiation," said Avery matter-of-factly. "Have you tried it?"

Maybe it was the alcohol or the fact that his companion, the trusted police officer was so persuasive that made Stimpson eventually agree to try the experience he recognised to be so dangerous. Even before he had agreed he saw Avery had been busy unpacking the remaining contents of his carrier bag. There was a long belt and what appeared to be a large pair of scissors that Avery carefully placed to one side as he moved the chair previously next to the desk into the centre of the room. With skilful dexterity Avery looped the belt over the high beam and adjusted the length of the loop that swayed menacingly below.

Sensing the Professor was about to sensibly change his mind, Avery kissed the older man and reassured him he would love what was to follow. Stimpson's elevated heart rate told him he would not, but at the same time he felt his free will had deserted him so he reluctantly stood on the chair as Avery looped the free end of the belt around his neck and instantly tightened it.

"Please be careful, Professor," said Avery as he took a few paces back and stood behind the sofa, using it as an improvised lectern. "You see, as the pressure from the belt cuts off the flow of blood through the veins in your neck it causes blood to congest in the brain. Oxygen levels drop as carbon dioxide levels increase and this will intensify your pleasure, but if it gets too much I always have my scissors handy for emergencies." He demonstrated a theatrical cut of an imaginary belt with the scissors to emphasise the point.

Stimpson was not feeling anything like pleasure as his hands moved up to loosen the noose.

"I don't like this, help me," he managed to gasp as he struggled to loosen the belt without affecting his balance on the chair.

"Oh of course, I'm so sorry," said Avery, rushing to offer assistance.

Relieved, Stimpson lowered his hands to allow Avery access to the belt. At that point in time Stimpson understood that after years of study of his specialist subject he was now in the presence of a psychopath. The pseudo face of concern had disappeared and Avery was now smiling as he casually lifted him from the chair and kicked it nonchalantly out of reach. For a moment there was no consequence as the two were locked in an embrace but as Avery extradited himself from the despairing grip of the Professor the belt immediately tightened further.

Avery returned to his informative lecture even though his audience had already lost consciousness.

"When death occurs, it's usually because of pressure on a part of the neck called the carotid body, a small cluster of chemoreceptors located near the fork of the carotid artery. Pressure on the carotid body causes a discharge from the vagus nerve. This slows down the heart and can make a person pass out instantaneously. Losing consciousness causes the person to go limp, which tightens the choke and decreases circulation through the neck arteries, causing asphyxiation. Rarely is there enough pressure to block the windpipe, rather, it's the lack of blood flow that causes death."

As Avery was speaking he carefully adjusted the crime scene to remove any indication of a second person's presence. This involved slightly adjusting the laptop's position and of course returning the washed second glass to the bathroom. In his experience the attending officers would have all the information they needed to determine this was an accidental death as a result of misadventure. After ensuring the corridor was clear Avery left the room using the same bouquet he had brought earlier to obscure his face as he exited into the busy London night. Although the pavement was crowded nobody prevented his brisk walk toward the West End. He wondered how much he would miss the anonymity of the big city.

But he was looking forward to returning home after serving his apprenticeship in the capital.

CHAPTER 12

Sean McKenzie had presumed he was going to be released at the same time as his elder brother so was somewhat surprised when he found out his liberty would come a full month ahead of Liam's. It was probably as a consequence of being the marginally better behaved sibling, he concluded as he tasted the celebratory beer his cousin had thoughtfully supplied upon picking him up at the prison gates.

"Do you want to go straight home, Sean?" asked the cousin as the car pulled onto the main road.

"No, not just yet, can we take a wee detour into the town?" smiled Sean, hoping his mother would forgive him for choosing to reunite with friends before family.

"A few of the boys are going to the Dragon, said we will meet them there," said the cousin whose preplanning suggested he knew Sean well.

*

"If the Devil could cast his net now, eh Sarge?" said the fresh-faced detective Bare had chosen to help him run the unofficial observation post. Steve Perkins was looking at the growing list of 'faces' arriving at the George and Dragon Public House via the telephoto lens on the camera Bare had provided. The pair had

54

secured access to an unoccupied office on the 4th floor of a building directly opposite the pub. The OP (Observation Post) wasn't ideal as the elevated vantage point meant they were looking down on the pub and could only see approximately a third of the adjoining car park. Still, it was better than using an unmarked car as had been Bare's original plan upon getting the tip-off about the 'Welcome Home' party two hours earlier. As Perkins took the photographs Bare jotted down the names of those he recognised on a piece of paper he had found in the otherwise empty office.

"I think there's a surveillance sheet in the boot of the car, Sarge, if you want me to go get it?" said the eager-to-please young detective.

"No, it's OK, we don't need one as this is just some casual intelligence gathering," explained Bare.

"But we still need…" Perkins' voice trailed off without finishing the sentence as he belatedly understood how 'unofficial' the observations were.

Bare had deliberately chosen the new detective to accompany him on the covert operation, in truth he would have rather done it by himself but experience had taught him it was difficult to handle all the equipment whilst monitoring the police radio in case his presence was needed elsewhere. As the sole supervisory detective on duty in the area strictly speaking he should not have been involved in any intelligence-gathering venture, authorised or not. It irked him though that since the robbery convictions the McKenzie crime syndicate had grown from strength to strength. Until his recent demise Stuart McKenzie had even legitimised his standing in the local community to the extent he was regularly featured in the local news as a generous benefactor to some or other charity. He had spoken publicly about the evils of alcohol and drugs, citing them as the cause of his sons being drawn into a world of criminality despite his best efforts to save them.

Yet all of Bare's intelligence sources, cultivated over years of detective graft, were telling him a very different story, painting a picture of ruthless organised crime. The Detective Sergeant had found the vast majority of his colleagues to be apathetic about securing a conviction against the McKenzies, put off no doubt by the previous investment of considerable hard work that never seemed to lead to a tangible result. Some bosses had even accused him of holding a personal vendetta against the family no doubt fuelled by the unsuccessful intimidation he and Morton had suffered in the lead up to the robbery trial. He knew that his friend shared his views but was frustrated that Morton would never 'rock the boat' for fear of it having a negative impact on his career. Julia had once suggested that Bare might consider adopting the same approach until her husband had cruelly retorted it was because she was more interested in the material proceeds an advancement of his career would offer her.

His growing conclusion was that no crime group were consistently that lucky without having some form of advantage. His intention was to gain as much intelligence as possible then seek an early appointment with his old friend Paul Avery and see if he had an appetite to investigate some suspected police corruption. By corruption of course he meant active collusion with high-level criminals rather than minor deviations from procedure and dodgy expense claims like the one he would have to create for the purchase of a camera and telephoto lens.

The arrival of Sean McKenzie at the pub could hardly have been missed by the surveilling officers. The waiting friends inside had clearly been given an advance warning of his approach and had hurriedly assembled outside to form some version of a guard of honour. The continuously sounding horn of the arriving car was answered by their cheers that were amplified further as McKenzie alighted from the car.

DC Perkins was in overdrive as he continuously depressed the button of the digital camera, not wanting to miss a single one of the succession of embraces that greeted the returning hero. Bare in contrast had stopped recording the names of criminal associates he had recognised and was instead staring at Sean McKenzie, amazed at how much prison had aged him. The long-haired athletic young man he had apprehended all those years ago had been replaced by a slightly younger version of his late father, complete with a receding hairline and a stomach that suggested prison food couldn't be that bad after all. If this was the younger, more handsome sibling he couldn't help but wonder what Liam now looked like.

Once the welcome party had returned into the pub Bare motioned to his partner that it was time to leave. They quietly left the building via a side exit that took them directly onto the quiet road where they had left the unmarked police vehicle. Bare noted with some amusement that the car that had been used to collect Sean, a black BMW, was now parked directly in front of theirs, presumably because the pub car park was full. It was a vehicle familiar to him as he had often observed Stuart McKenzie driving it around town in what he considered to be an overt show of wealth and social standing. Whilst Perkins busied himself putting their equipment away in the boot of the CID car Bare took childish delight in surreptitiously using his key to deeply scratch the entire nearside length of the shiny status symbol.

CHAPTER 13

The new Detective Superintendent experienced a much more sombre welcome as he walked back into the police station he had left as a competent but unremarkable Police Constable some years earlier. Although the building had changed very little it seemed so much smaller than Avery remembered. He momentarily doubted his decision to accept the promotion, wondering whether he had outgrown the familiar surroundings when he saw a familiar face striding toward him.

"Good to see you back, boss," said Morton.

"Good to see you too, Jim," said Avery, delighted that his newly acquired rank had been so readily accepted by his old friend. "Congratulations on making DI," he added, subtlety reinforcing his own greater achievement.

The pair shared the lift to the top floor so that Avery could drop off his briefcase in his new office before embarking on a nostalgic tour of the building with Morton acting as guide. Following numerous introductions and pleasantries they arrived at the station canteen which was sparsely populated; the lunch service had ended minutes earlier.

Avery saw the third musketeer sitting at a table with a much younger colleague examining the photographic footage they had captured earlier.

"Sebastian, so nice to see you again," said Avery, extending his hand by way of simultaneous greeting.

Bare ignored the confused expression on Perkins' face which had greeted the proclamation of his first name as he stood up to provide a firm handshake.

"Great to have you back, Paul."

DC Perkins, unable to cope with the sudden influx of senior officers, made his excuses and left as soon as was able leaving the three friends to catch up over a coffee. They chatted for an hour, each man in turn providing a brief synopsis of their life both personal and professional that had occurred since they had last been together. The junior officers used the opportunity to informally brief their new boss about the current crime trends in the area as Bare attempted to weigh up how 'corporate' his old friend had become. It was a common phenomenon he had observed that those who achieved Inspector or above seemed to disassociate themselves from the 'real world' where he operated with a largely unappreciated efficiency.

Avery smiled inwardly as the challenges the officers described seemed so inconsequential to those he had faced on a daily basis in London. The murder rate in his absence had barely exceeded his personal tally and he was unable to resist his own personal theatre as Morton informed him there was only one on the books that had not been detected.

"You must remember it, Simon Vickers," said Morton, repeating the victim's name.

Avery looked up and to the right, feigning classic recall pose before saying, "Vaguely, wasn't it gang related?"

"Yes, that's the one," said Morton, reinforcing the incorrect hypothesis of the Senior Investigating Officer involved who had since retired.

"I think it was down to the McKenzies," added Bare, continuing his tradition of habitually blaming the crime family for any unsolved misdemeanour. "He had done some dealing for them in the past," he added to counter Morton's raised eyebrows with the most tenuous of intelligence snippets he had once received from a 'source'.

"It's good to hear that vendetta is alive and well," laughed Avery.

"It is, though Stuart McKenzie isn't," quipped Morton, pleased with his rare comic timing.

Bare was pleased to exploit the early reference to the McKenzies and added he had 'heard' that the younger son had been released.

"Is that an issue for you two?" enquired Avery. "I remember there were threats in the lead up to the trial."

"I don't think so, boss," replied Morton. "Over the last few years I met Stuart at lots of social occasions and he actually felt we had done the boys a favour by nicking them when we did before they got themselves killed."

Avery noted it was Bare's turn to raise his eyebrows and felt something akin to genuine affection for both men. Much to Bare's frustration the conversation moved onto other matters and he felt any further attempt to talk again about the Scottish family would indeed make him sound like he was on a personal crusade. Whilst Morton was ordering three further coffees at the counter Avery took the opportunity to gently remind Bare that he needed to use the term 'sir' or 'boss' in front of junior colleagues. The rebuke had caused Bare to retreat into a sullen silence for the remainder of their discussion, his view firmly reaffirmed that Avery had moved to the 'dark side'.

"Anyway, you shouldn't use the term 'unsolved murders' as a

performance indicator, it assumes there are no undiscovered bodies buried in the woods or that all missing persons are alive and well whereas a proportion may have encountered a grisly end," preached Avery, drawing from the advanced teachings of his former employer.

Bare grimaced at the instruction of how to suck eggs and looked for an exit strategy.

His excuse to leave was to catch the attractive brunette walking out of the canteen en route back to the typing pool where Bare wanted her to prioritise some of his work.

"Exit pursued by a Bare," laughed Avery as Morton looked at him blankly.

"It's from The Winter's Tale," explained Doris to Morton as the elderly canteen worker collected the empty cups from the table long after Avery had also departed. "He's a very clever man, your new boss but I wouldn't trust him, his eyes are too close together," added the astute judge of character.

CHAPTER 14

Julia Bare's Monday morning started alone in bed. The empty other half of the King-Size Deluxe proffered no clues as to the whereabouts of her husband. In the early days, if she had ever woken alone, there would have been a note on his pillow. Rarely romantic, often comical, but enough to make her feel loved until she saw him again. Like a fix to the addicts she had previously dealt with on a daily basis, she had become hooked and wholly dependent on him. And therein lay the problem because the thing that drew Bare to Julia so passionately was her free spirit and glorious independence.

Of course there were a myriad of contributing factors to the decline in their relationship. The repeated failures to have children and the subsequent miscarriage being, perhaps, the most obvious causes. In the early days of their marriage, there had been no conscious decision to increase the Bare family, just a belief in the inevitable, but when Julia failed to get pregnant, the pressure to do so became immense. The Bares no longer made love, instead engaging in a clinical act with only one objective. When a seemingly endless procession of medical experts could find no physical reason for her failure to conceive, Julia was left with the well-meaning advice of friends, to just relax and it would eventually happen. Not so easy when she suspected that Sebastian was getting his relaxation elsewhere. The ecstasy of a positive indication on a home pregnancy test had lasted a precious few weeks before Julia miscarried.

Physically, the healing process had been relatively speedy but her mental recovery was slow and painful. She felt a different person, as if her identity had been stolen from her. Although it had not been said, she sensed that Sebastian blamed her but she couldn't rationalise exactly for what. Whilst she would have declared herself still to be merely a social drinker, her husband and the local bottle bank knew otherwise. She was a mess. The extended career break turned into a resignation after she had been forced to admit she no longer possessed the confidence needed to be an effective police officer.

Friends had been initially supportive whilst Julia waited for time to be the great healer. However, as one by one they drifted away she reached the conclusion that nothing would ever be the same. This gave her the determination to climb out of the bottle.

Life with Sebastian had become difficult but despite her suspicions, she was not looking for a confession, choosing to believe that the changes she saw in him were mirror images of her own depression and not through unhappiness with his home life and her. And so, Sebastian and Julia Bare had remained together, defying the popular view amongst friends and colleagues that their respective track records pointed towards an intense yet brief affair rather than a protracted marriage.

Part of her daily ritual was to study the silver-framed wedding photograph standing on the landing table as she walked towards the bathroom. Once prominently displayed for all to see, its position now was the result of one of many therapeutic decluttering exercises. Julia desperately tried to recognise the laughing bride with her sparking eyes and effortless grace but they were now only distant relatives. The bathroom mirror confirmed further evidence of stress and the passing of time, in spite of the array of expensive pots of creams and lotions set out on the clinical, white-tiled window sill like a promotional display in a beauty salon.

As the jets from the power shower stimulated her body she felt refreshed. She smiled inwardly as the memory of the first shower she had shared with Sebastian involuntarily entered her thoughts. She remembered it as a truly intense experience and whilst accepting it as the distant memory it was, she saw it as an indication that her feelings for him were not completely cold and she was pleasantly surprised to leave the bathroom in a more optimistic frame of mind. She made a mental list of the positives in her life and now considered today's job interview amongst them. Perhaps today would mark a change in her fortunes.

After spending an inordinate amount of time drying her hair, applying her make-up and thereby sacrificing a breakfast, Julia left the house and drove the short distance into the town centre. The bright sun made her curse the absence of her sunglasses, left in a moment of alcohol-induced forgetfulness at the races ten days earlier. She also began to regret her choice of grey trouser suit for the interview but immediately chastised herself for allowing negativity to again creep into her thought processes. This was to be her first job interview since leaving the police and the last one ever in her relatively short life.

CHAPTER 15

Mary McKenzie never made the same mistake twice. She again checked her watch as she sat in the rear of the new Range Rover waiting impatiently for her son to emerge from what her driver had assured her was the exit used for releasing prisoners. The driver had been in the McKenzies' employ for several years but still remained nervous in the company of the 'black widow'. The recently attributed nickname suited her well but he pitied anyone who might vocalise it aloud.

"It shouldn't be long now, Mrs McKenzie, it will be great to have Liam home too," he said to break the silence of their wait.

The glowered silent response from the rear seat was a good indication that small talk was still firmly off the menu. He knew how angry she had been with Sean's late arrival the previous month, taking it as a sign of disrespect that he chosen a drinking session with his mates over family. She was clearly not going to afford Liam the same opportunity.

Mary was also thinking about Sean's homecoming and the lecture she had given her fragile son over breakfast the morning after his intoxicated return.

"With your father gone there will be people looking to see if we are weak and vulnerable, there are vultures circling our business," she had told him.

"They wouldn't dare," had been her hungover son's mumbled response.

So she had led him outside like a naughty schoolboy in full view of everyone and pointed to the very evident damage on her late husband's car.

"Nobody would have dared do that when Stuart was alive."

Despite his protestations it was just 'kids' responsible Mary had used the existence of the criminal damage to remind her family and staff they needed to be on their guard.

"We tolerate nothing that disrespects the family," she had said with a great deal of conviction, allowing her steely gaze to linger slightly longer on Shannon McKenzie. Now as Shannon's husband belatedly emerged from the side gate she prepared to give him the same lecture.

Whilst Liam had understood his mother's personal chauffeur service he had considered it completely unnecessary. Unlike his younger brother he had no wish to delay being reunited with his family. He felt nervous about how Cameron would receive the father he barely knew despite his mother's assurances that the boy had literally been counting the days since learning of his imminent release. His own father's death had led to extended periods of sombre reflection whilst staring at the dirty yellow ceiling of his cell. Fellow inmates had known better than attempting to cajole Liam away from the comfort of his bunk and even the previously antagonistic guards had given him the maximum amount of space prison allows.

He stared out of the car window, lost in his own thoughts and not even taking in the novelty views of expansive unfenced countryside as it flashed past. He knew that it was destiny to lead the family just as his father had done for so many years before. Equally he knew that he was not yet equipped to do so, his mother commanded more respect and knew the intimate detail of the business that had no doubt evolved further in his absence. But this was a new version of Liam McKenzie, more mature, more considered and certainly much more focused, he vowed to himself. There was a burning question, however, that now he was free from the paranoia of covert listening devices he could at last ask aloud.

"So why has the family never done anything about Bare and Morton?" he asked his mother. Even the mention of their names brought back the vivid image of Detective Constable Bare giving him a surreptitious wink as the brothers had been led handcuffed from the dock post-sentence.

"It was your da's decision. I thought for years it was because he didn't want to start a war we couldn't win," explained Mary.

There was clearly more to expand on but Mary's subtle glance in the driver's direction told Liam the rest would have to come when they were completely alone.

"Just tell me it's not over," he whispered and her response of a smile and a reassuring touch of his arm told him it wasn't.

CHAPTER 16

It had taken James Morton several years to fully understand and even grudgingly appreciate the sophistication and execution of the entrapment operation that had ensnared him. Like his friend Sebastian Bare he had suffered numerous clumsy attempts to intimidate him prior to the McKenzie brothers' trial. These had only served to strengthen his resolve to present his evidence at the Crown Court in a professional and detailed manner. The pair had received a Judge's commendation for their bravery in apprehending the robbers, an honour rarely bestowed on young, inexperienced detectives. The accolade had served him well over the years as all his applications had modestly included it to demonstrate there was a lot more to the studious applicant than met the eye.

But after the trial, possibly with his guard down, he had joined the team for a social night out to celebrate the convictions. At Bare's insistence the large group of detectives had gone to Roxy's nightclub as their final destination of their local hostelries tour. The collective alcohol intake of the group undoubtedly influenced their risk assessment of wildly celebrating in a club part owned by Stuart McKenzie. It was also frequented by virtually every face in the rogues gallery displayed on the wall in the CID office. Surprisingly the off-duty police officers had encountered no problems, a fact that proved the war had been won according to Bare during a drunken embrace.

Even though Morton was enjoying the occasion he found himself on the periphery of the revellers, preferring to observe rather than immerse himself totally in the celebrations. As he sipped his drink he saw the stunning young woman standing at the bar smiling in his direction. This was a rare occurrence for Morton and his initial instinct was to look around to see the real intended recipient of the smile. Predictably Bare was standing next to him and immediately responded to the smile by striding purposefully over toward the woman. The deafening noise of the music being played in the club made it impossible to hear even a shouted remark with any clarity but the body language of Bare and his intended conquest indicated the initial greeting had not gone well. After the briefest of encounters he had observed Bare shrug his shoulders in resignation and return to the ironic cheers of his colleagues. Morton had enjoyed the sight of a rare rebuttal for his friend and found himself uncharacteristically raising his class in a distanced gesture of admiration. To his utter amazement the gesture was mirrored by the female whose accompanying head tilt indicated he should go over to her. Within moments he was chatting to Teagen, having established her unusual name at the third time of asking and had even managed to order a couple of drinks at the incredibly busy bar. As the couple made their way hand in hand to the dance floor Morton had received a couple of congratulatory winks from colleagues who were busily ridiculing Bare for losing his lothario crown. Morton had of course apologised for his friend's boorish behaviour although was secretly loving his time in the spotlight. During the softer music that accompanied the ritual slow dances toward the end of the evening Teagen had told him she worked part-time at the club. She had at first doubted Morton and his friends were police officers but after he had convinced her, she had appeared genuinely impressed.

During the last dance before the club was due to close Morton had managed to summon the courage to briefly kiss her and to his delight Teagen instantly reciprocated with a much longer and passionate meeting of lips. Then as the music stopped they found themselves awkwardly illuminated by the harsh main lights of the club which was the clear signal it was about to close. Bare came over to them and asked if the couple were going to join him and the rest of the group for a late-night visit to a takeaway. Morton looked to Teagen for guidance before quickly opting for her alternate suggestion of remaining at the club for a staff-entitled after-hours drink. So Bare and the remaining group left the pair after advising them not to 'do anything he wouldn't do.' Morton felt this meant he had pretty much free range to embark on any activity given his friend's experience in such matters.

After sharing an intimate drink, Teagen had led him to a store room at the rear of the club where despite the unsuited surroundings they had the best sex Morton had ever experienced. Afterwards she had coyly shown him the rear door where he was able to make a discreet exit away from the view of the remaining club employees who were clearing up inside. With Teagen's number safely in his pocket Morton enjoyed the walk home through the brightly lit but deserted streets of the town.

*

The next morning he had fielded the odd question from a curious colleague with a knowing smile that he had witnessed Bare use on countless occasions before. Disappointingly his friend had not asked for a chapter and verse account of what had happened after they had parted the night before, but he attributed this to Bare's obvious hangover rather than a lack of curiosity. Morton had already decided he was going to play it decidedly cool in any case as he hoped that his brief meeting with Teagen would flourish into something much more. He had attempted to call her a couple of times but the number she had provided was unanswered which he hoped meant she was having a lay in rather than ignoring him.

When his own phone rang that afternoon he was surprised when the male caller identified himself as Stuart McKenzie. He had never spoken to the convicted robber's father before and was astonished at how articulate and pleasant the man appeared to be. Even more bizarre was the fact that the notorious hardcase was apparently thanking the Constabulary for locking up his sons and saving them from an inevitable life of self-destruction fuelled by drugs. The conversation had ended after Mr McKenzie had requested a personal meeting that he felt would be 'mutually beneficial'. The caller had stressed he only wished to speak privately to Morton and had no wish to engage with his partner Bare who he had observed during the trial, considering him to be unprofessional. Morton was aware of intelligence surrounding the McKenzies but rationalised that the man who had called him had no previous convictions. In truth he was also not used to having his ego massaged and had rarely if ever been favourably compared to his partner. He therefore agreed to meet for a coffee in a local hotel close to the police station.

Confident that he wasn't breaching any police protocols and with the security of the meeting being in a public place Morton set off for the hotel. As he departed the CID office he told Bare he was going to meet a potential intelligence source but his partner's only response was to ask him if he could pick up some paracetamol on the way back.

Stuart McKenzie was already seated in the corner of the coffee lounge waiting for Morton's arrival. He was smartly dressed and the designer suit he was wearing highlighted the disparity in his and the young Detective's wealth. He greeted the arrival of the younger man with a warm handshake and thanked him for making time to meet. As Morton sipped the coffee bought in advance of his arrival he listened intently as McKenzie repeated the sentiment of the earlier phone conversation.

"You see DC Morton, family means everything to me and I guess I have known for a while that Liam and Sean have been going a bit off the rails, I can't condone what they did and I am just thankful nobody got hurt during the robbery, but I know it was drugs at the root of this, do you see?"

Morton had nodded but wasn't entirely sure where the conversation was heading. By way of explanation McKenzie had gone on to intimate that whilst he ran a legitimate business he often became aware of information about illegal drug supply which he wanted to pass on.

"But I will only talk to someone I can trust, DC Morton," emphasised McKenzie, "which is why I wouldn't want to discuss anything with that gobshite partner of yours."

Morton had realised that it was probably futile to defend Bare at that stage so simply ignored the latter comment before explaining in detail the rules and regulations pertaining to police informants. He had told McKenzie that if the relationship were to go forward that there was specific legislation in place designed to protect all those involved, including the requirement for two officers to be present during any future meetings. He could tell immediately from the expression on the gruff Scotsman's face that he was not receptive to that.

And then it happened.

"Okay son, I will think about what you said, but before you go I need to discuss something a bit delicate," said McKenzie whilst simultaneously reaching into his inside jacket pocket.

Morton was initially relieved that the hand didn't reappear with a gun but instead saw that McKenzie was passing him a photograph. The Detective instinctively took the picture and saw that it was of a young girl dressed in school uniform. At first he didn't recognise her, fresh faced and devoid of any make up.

"I think you know my wee niece Teagen, don't you Jim?" said McKenzie, confirming Morton's belated recognition of the girl.

The rest of the conversation had been a bit of a blur for Morton who was desperate to leave the hotel but was paralysed by a rising feeling of dread that something very bad was happening. McKenzie explained that his 15-year-old niece was down from Scotland on her school holidays and had been employed to wash glasses at his nightclub for some extra pocket money. He had become concerned about the way she had presented when he had picked her up from the club at closing time the previous night. Following a tip-off from a bar worker he had checked the CCTV footage from the store room and had witnessed the reason for her preoccupation.

Morton had listened in silence to the monotone commentary before desperately telling McKenzie that he had believed Teagen to be at least ten years older.

"Aye, it's shameful the way these lassies dress, but you see my dilemma Jim when I recognised you on the recording, I mean my brother would rip your balls off if he knew."

Morton had been contemplating criminal charges and in truth the potential for physical injury had not even occurred to him but he drew some comfort in McKenzie's reassuring tone.

"The way I see it, Jim, is that one minor indiscretion shouldn't define a man's life, we are both men of the world and nobody else needs to know about this, the girl's going back to Scotland and she won't say anything so we can keep this between you and me, our secret, eh?"

With a friendly tap on the Detective's shoulder McKenzie stood up and picked up the bill that had been left on their table. "I'll get this, son, you can get the next one." And then he was gone leaving Morton alone with his thoughts.

He heard nothing for several weeks and it was almost a relief when McKenzie finally got in contact again. It had started with minor things that were not even necessarily illegal, akin to a friend ringing a police officer for advice. He of course had no option but to provide the information requested that gradually escalated to the supply of sensitive information from police databases. In return he actually received useful criminal intelligence, mainly about competitors that McKenzie wished to see inconvenienced by police action. Morton had in fact devised a clever way of introducing this information into the intelligence database whilst disguising its origin as an anonymous source.

Despite Morton trying in later years to distance himself from operational policing and thereby become of less use, McKenzie always found a way to him, even using him as a means to become accepted as a freemason. Thereafter McKenzie made it clear that his only expectation was that he never wished to be surprised by the Constabulary so he was always told about any planned operations against his family.

Teagen McKenzie was never mentioned again although Stuart did let slip years later at some drunken masonic function that neither he nor his brothers had ever had a daughter.

CHAPTER 17

Bare sat alone in the coffee shop awaiting his wife's arrival. He checked his watch and wondered what the reason for the delay was. Her interview was surely over by now and the firm of solicitors seeking a new administrator was only a few blocks away. He checked his phone for any missed calls or additions to the text she had sent him earlier but there was no new information waiting for him. He had been confused by her text suggesting a coffee after her interview as surely a debrief could have waited until he had finished work but it was such an out-of-character request he had felt compelled to comply.

After another flat white she appeared in the doorway and he was happy to see how good she looked. The doubts she had expressed for days about the futility of applying for the job had clearly given way to a determination that he remembered from their early times together. The familiar comic exaggerated point to his watch signalled his position amongst the crowd of caffeine junkies and she quickly made her way over to the window booth.

As she sat down he immediately stood intending to join the long queue to buy his wife a coffee and replenish his own but she motioned for him to sit down. The excitement so evident in her eyes confused Bare and he could only think of one explanation.

"You obviously got the job," he smiled, anticipating her proud announcement.

"I think I probably did," replied Julia, "but I may have to turn it down," her voice full of excitement.

Bare's face accurately reflected his confusion and Julia was unable to contain her secret any longer as she handed him the item that had been concealed in her hand. He had seen many pregnancy test kits in their marriage but was still struggling to interpret the positive indication it was displaying.

"I thought it was just pre-interview nerves, me feeling sick for the last few days but I did the test in the solicitor's toilet while I was waiting to get called in," she laughed. "I have no idea what they asked me in the interview," she added with glee.

For an astute detective it took a disproportionate amount of time for Bare to process the information he was receiving from the test indicator and his pregnant wife. Finally his facial expression changed from confusion to joy.

"You clever, clever girl," he said and the pair stood simultaneously and embraced each therewith, neither wanting to break first and lose the moment.

They left the coffee shop and walked hand in hand to the nearest pub where Bare theatrically ordered a large red wine for himself and an orange juice for Julia despite her protestations she wanted something stronger to celebrate.

"No alcohol for you, pregnant woman," he said, returning to the table with the two glasses. "And none for me either," added the on-duty officer as he swapped the glasses' position on the table.

Julia's mystified look quickly disappeared as she realised that the man approaching them was her husband's new boss.

"So this is where my Detective Sergeant spends his time fighting crime," said Avery.

"Just on my lunch break, Paul," said Bare. "You remember Julia, don't you?"

"Yes of course, how are you Julia?" enquired Avery whilst leaning forward to kiss her cheek.

"Am great, thanks," she replied honestly. "Will you join us, Paul? It's been ages and congratulations so much on your promotions."

"Sadly am just leaving, only popped in for a quick one with the ACC," said Avery, nodding toward a well-dressed man standing in awkward isolation by the front door. "Let's all catch up soon. Enjoy your lunch, Seb," he said before departing after what Bare considered to be another unnecessary kiss on Julia's cheek.

Bare waited for the men to leave before swapping the drinks back to their original position even though Julia had taken a mischievous sip of wine during her greeting of Avery.

"He hasn't changed much," she said.

"Yeah he has, he's had the corporate chip inserted," replied Bare.

"I wasn't talking about his career, the man's a creep, none of the girls trusted him back in the day," said Julia.

Before she could expand on the comments she was interrupted by her phone ringing and the pair struggled to contain their laughter as she was formally offered the position of Office Administrator.

CHAPTER 18

It was like any other boardroom meeting with the senior managers waiting for the arrival of the Chief Executive Officer. When she arrived Mary McKenzie noted that her youngest son was the only absentee from the hastily convened family meeting. She was about to question the others about his whereabouts when Sean's entrance via the kitchen door answered the question. He was still eating a bacon roll so could only raise his free hand by way of apology for his late arrival.

Mary was the only woman in the room and took her normal seat at the head of the large rectangular dining room table. She was flanked by her two sons but despite her slight stature there was no doubt in the other eight family members' minds who was in charge.

"Thank you all for finding time to come," she began with no acknowledgement that her summons had provided them with little choice in the matter. "I wanted to take the opportunity to thank you all for the support you have given me since Stuart died. It means a lot."

She paused long enough to allow any of the family to respond but was met only by solemn deferential nods around the table. So she continued her opening address.

"And obviously it's great to have Liam and Sean back home, so I want everyone to know where we are at."

Mary then went into detail about the new management structure she was imposing. Essentially the McKenzie family had a portfolio of legitimate business interests that had evolved over time under the stewardship of her late husband. These included a modestly sized haulage company, a prestige car dealership and a nightclub. The haulage company had two operating bases, the main one being close to the McKenzie residence and the other in Scotland where a number of the extended family resided. Although Stuart had appointed family members as managers he had always resisted relinquishing control beyond that. The McKenzies used their legitimate business interests to mask criminal activities that included drugs importation and supply. Such was the scale of their operation the main challenge to Stuart had been to legitimise or 'launder' the considerable income the illicit activities were generating. He had found that this was an increasingly complex challenge and had felt vulnerable as law enforcement agencies seemed to be increasingly 'chasing the money' as they tackled organised crime. For that reason whilst his own sons were serving their custodial sentences Stuart had invested heavily in the education of his eldest nephew, Patrick McKenzie, who was now the family official accountant. This had turned out to be the perfect career choice for the studious nephew who enjoyed the trappings of wealth that the family business brought him but had no appetite for the bloodlust necessary to work on the frontline.

Mary had a lot of time for Patrick which irritated her sons who didn't fully appreciate their cousin's worth. He in turn disliked the prodigal sons and was relieved to hear at the meeting that Mary was to remain in place as his main point of contact. In fact all the family members were reassured that the main message being conveyed was very much 'business as usual'.

After listening without comment for the duration of the

meeting Liam sought clarification around his and Sean's role. Mary carefully explained that it was their destiny to one day take over the reins but only when she was satisfied they had the maturity and expertise to do it.

"Aye, it's what Stuart would have wanted," said Patrick's father in support of his sister-in-law.

Liam was not surprised at the proposal and understood the rationale behind it, in fact he was largely content with everything that had been discussed but had one pressing item under 'any other business?'

"What about the bastard that locked me up?" he motioned.

Mary placed the fountain pen she had been revolving in her fingers down on the table knowing that her next comment was not going to be well received by either of her sons but especially Liam.

"I discussed that with your da before he died. We have an asset in the Constabulary and don't want to jeopardise the business by pursuing a personal vendetta so they are off limits," she said coldly whilst looking at her eldest son, directly into his defiant eyes.

"What asset?" he asked.

Mary turned to provide her answer to the whole family.

"Stuart turned a cop and for years only me and him knew who it was. I will share the name with my sons in private but I will be the only one who ever contacts him just as Stuart was the only one before. You just need to know the arrangement, provided it's handled correctly, affords the family some protection, so don't make waves, OK?"

There was a murmur of agreement in the room as well as an affirmation that Stuart had really been a clever old bastard.

CHAPTER 19

It had not been his most lucrative day. Sometimes some passing generous soul would place a note in his paper cup but today there were only coins and most of those were a depressing copper colour. Jack considered changing his location to somewhere with a higher footfall but he had grown accustomed to the relative sanctuary of the doorway of the long-since-closed shop. When he saw the two smartly dressed men emerge from the pub next door he shuffled forward in anticipation. Depending on their alcohol intake lunching businessmen could either be incredibly generous or intolerant to the homeless but it was always worth a go.

"Any spare change, sirs?" he asked and extended the white cup that was in stark contrast to his dirty hand.

The first man recoiled at the sudden and clearly unwelcome request but the second man stopped and encouragingly removed his wallet from his jacket pocket.

'There you go, mate," Avery said handing the homeless one a crisp ten-pound note.

Jack took the note quickly before the man changed his mind or just cruelly withdrew it as had happened on many other encounters. Only then did he look up to see the face of his benefactor and at this point it was his turn to involuntarily recoil.

"Thank you very much, sir," he managed to mumble whilst averting his eyes from Avery.

The two men walked briskly away and he heard them say something about how terribly sad it was to see an old man begging. No doubt they had also assumed he was suffering from mental health issues, Jack thought. But there was nothing wrong with his brain and even though he had not seen that face for several years he was certain that his memory was accurate. That was the policeman he had observed whilst sleeping rough in the Mariners Arms, a memory he had never shared as he had no wish to end up locked in a car boot too.

*

It had been a productive lunch for Avery. His view was that any interaction with a senior officer should be viewed as a promotion board and had treated the invitation to dine with ACC Kent accordingly. On the surface it was a relaxed and informal pub lunch but Avery knew that he had scored points throughout having researched the career profile of Kent. Senior police officers can't help but recruit people in their own image so Avery had positioned himself as a highly ambitious performance-orientated officer. He knew the ACC was keen to win brownie points from the Home Office for effectively tackling organised crime and had dropped all the current buzz words into casual conversation. The pair shared the previous experience of working in the Metropolitan Police and Avery correctly sensed this had caused Kent to be slightly patronising concerning the challenges of more rural policing. By the time they had consumed their meal Avery was pretty sure that despite being the new kid in town he would have no problems in securing the next rank in a relatively short time. He couldn't have scripted the walk back to the police station better as the pair had been accosted by some tramp which allowed him to demonstrate his empathy with the vulnerable.

Upon his return to his office Avery began considering how to advance the promises he had made to Kent over lunch. It was okay 'talking the talk' but rhetoric only lasted in the memory so long and he would need to produce something tangible to keep the ACC in his fan club. His impromptu meeting with the Bares reminded him that Sebastian had been seeking a private meeting to talk about the McKenzie family. He wasn't convinced that the family presented much of a problem since the demise of Stuart but there again he wasn't really up to speed with local issues as yet. His recollection of Bare from their early days together was that he had a good nose for such things so maybe he was onto something. He decided to at least hear what Sebastian had to say and asked his secretary to set up a meeting. He could of course have contacted the Sergeant himself but subtle things like a third-party summons reinforced the fact they were no longer equal. It had been nice to see Julia again, however, reflected Avery. He had no doubt that had he not transferred to the Met shortly after her arrival that the two would have dated. As he again took time to take in the view from his office window he smiled at the assumption that Julia would be berating herself for settling on Bare now that the better man was back in town.

CHAPTER 20

The initial excitement of discovering the identity of their 'friend' in the police quickly subsided as Mary McKenzie stipulated the strict operating protocols to her sons. She explained how their father had sustained the relationship by never pushing it too far and she was going to adopt the same principle.

She could tell from their reaction she had made the right call, demonstrating trust in them by allowing them some knowledge but not allowing them to be overly 'hands on'. She was confident that both respected her enough not to challenge her authority but her mother's intuition told her they both needed close management. To that end she had given them each specific responsibilities in the knowledge they would be kept busy and engaged.

Satisfied the pair had been appropriately briefed she retreated alone to the small study. She inserted a new SIM card into the safe 'burner' phone and dialled the number she had memorised. She heard the ringtone repeat several times before the personalised voicemail kicked in. She immediately depressed the red button to terminate the call surmising that the recipient was too busy to answer. It was only the second time she had attempted to contact Morton and she was a patient woman.

Morton had almost answered the withheld caller number but had sensed who was on the other end of the line so let it ring out. The lack of a voicemail message indicated he had probably been right. Frustratingly he had almost grown to trust Stuart McKenzie who had always reassured him that it was in their mutual interest to keep their relationship exclusive. As the days passed after Stuart's death he had slowly become more confident that the burden of his duplicitous role had been lifted forever. Without understanding the reason behind it his wife had also become buoyed by her unusually happy and carefree husband. Then he had received that call from Mary McKenzie. Just like her late husband, her tone had been measured and even friendly but that only served to somehow heighten the dread that was now evolving into a weary resignation. She had told him that Stuart spoke highly of their 'friendship' and she hoped it could continue. Morton had been noncommittal in his answer but they both knew he had no choice.

Despite trying to think of endless exit strategies Morton had yet to come up with a plan that didn't end up with him in prison or doing a moonlight flit to Spain. He knew by not answering his phone he was deferring the problem but at least he would be a day closer to his retirement. His thought were interrupted by Bare entering the office after the most cursory of knocks on his door. Even though he had achieved a higher rank Morton continued to aspire to be Bare. He had a presence about him that other men envied and women always seemed to love him however badly he appeared to treat them.

"Got a minute, Jim?" asked Bare, taking no sign of an immediate rebuttal as a cue to sit down.

"For you, Sebastian, always," Morton replied, bracing himself for whatever problem Bare was bringing to him. Experience had told him that Bare enjoyed full autonomy in his work until the proverbial wheel had come off or at least was furiously wobbling.

"Avery wants to see me," said Bare flatly.

"I'm not sure if that's a statement or question?" said a genuinely confused Morton.

"Do you know what it's about?" asked Bare, displaying a slight irritation that his enquiry had been ambiguous.

"No idea, mate," said Morton. And then as an afterthought, "Why, what have you done this time?"

Bare shifted uncomfortably but didn't answer his supervisor's question, instead preferring another statement.

"DC Perkins went to see him earlier."

"Yes I know, it was to get his detective probationary period signed off," said Morton, struggling to understand the correlation.

"Oh yeah, I had forgotten about that," replied Bare with a relieved puff of his cheeks that only served to confuse Morton further.

"Well I best not keep the 'special one' waiting," said an already departing Bare before he could be rebuked for promoting the nickname that was already in common use in the station canteen.

Reassured that he could think of nothing else that the 'special one' may wish to discuss with him in terms of misconduct Bare entered the secretary's office that was adjacent to Avery's. Ann was an authoritative figure in her early 60s who had worked for a succession of Detective Superintendents although many had later conceded they had often felt like she was actually training them. Although she would never admit it she enjoyed her reputation as a fearsome protector of the position much like the stereotypical doctor's receptionist one typically encounters. Her relationship with Bare, however, was somewhat unique; he had long since seen through her austere exterior and she was now very much the Miss Moneypenny to his James Bond.

"You been a bad boy again, Sebastian?" she teased but resisted the opportunity to look up from her terribly important work.

"You tell me," he replied, already standing next to her and playfully examining the contents of her boss's in-tray until he felt the inevitable slap of his hand.

"Well you are always bad, but I haven't had time to train this one yet so I guess you will have to go find out yourself," she said, regretting it would signal the end of her flirtatious interlude. "Make yourself useful and take this in for him," she added, handing him a binder containing the day's performance reports.

"Ah, perfect," said Bare. "I will put it down my trousers ready for my beating."

"Am sure that won't be necessary, Sergeant," said Avery from the open doorway causing Ann's heart to miss a beat having failed to observe his presence.

Once inside the office Bare was relieved to discover none of his misdemeanours were on the agenda. There was a fleeting reference to the meeting in the pub but only in terms of how well Julia was looking rather than any criticism of being in a licensed premises on duty. Bare had already prepared a defence for that in any case, although he had always thought its use to be a remote possibility given the fact that Avery and the ACC were in the same establishment themselves.

The pleasant surprise of learning Avery actually wanted to discuss the McKenzies made the junior officer actually regret devising and circulating the 'special one' nickname around the station. Although he had smiled upon hearing the mutation of the name to 'the special needs one' he might now have to actually challenge that if said in his presence, he reflected.

He spoke virtually uninterrupted for nearly an hour as Avery made notes about the composition of the family and their many business interests. He had tried to remain balanced but often his enthusiasm got the better of him as he speculated about the depth and complexity of their criminality. He saw that on those occasions Avery's pen had stopped writing, making it clear the senior officer was really only interested in correlated facts rather than wild hypotheses.

As he concluded he looked to Avery for some sign of affirmation but the man's face was a blank canvass.

After a pause to allow the received information to assimilate Avery delivered his verdict.

"I can't lie, I am a bit disappointed, we don't appear to have ever got close to them," the Detective Superintendent concluded, now privately wondering whether he had been rash in his promises to the ACC.

"But that's my point, Paul, they cannot be consistently this lucky, someone must be helping them," emphasised Bare, frustrated that his assertion was not as blindingly obvious to Avery.

'Well in the Met it was commonplace for Organised Crime Groups to attempt to infiltrate the police," conceded Avery, "but I am going to need more before I call in the Anti-Corruption Team, and if and when I do we had better be watertight on everything we have done," he added.

"I wasn't thinking about the soft shoe squad, Paul," said Bare who had no wish to be subjected to their fabled level of scrutiny. "Just let me set up a standalone small team, hand-picked and working on a secure separate intelligence system so we can be confident there are no leaks."

Avery leaned back in his leather chair and considered the suggestion. Politically it would play better if he could deliver a result without the assistance of an outside department and despite his reservations Bare's briefing had actually been quite compelling.

"OK, you can pick four detectives, an Intelligence Development officer and an Analyst, I will square it with Jim Morton, but I want everything by the book, no shortcuts, OK?"

'Blimey Paul, it's not the Met, I was only going to ask for DC Perkins," said Bare with inadvertent honesty.

"Okay, I will leave it to you," said Avery, flustered that he had not yet adjusted to the resourcing profile of a provincial Force. "I will call in a favour from London and am sure I will get you access to a dedicated financial investigator."

After blowing a departing kiss to Ann, Bare immediately returned to Morton's office to tell him of his assignment from Avery. Such was his happiness at being given the role he didn't notice the somewhat downbeat endorsement of the Detective Inspector who shortly afterwards decided to finish early for the day.

As he drove toward the sanctuary of the golf club Morton received another withheld call but on this occasion he elected to answer it.

"How have you been, Jim?" enquired the woman, her Scottish accent seeming even more pronounced on the car hands-free speaker.

"Yes, fine, I think we really need to meet, Mary, it's all getting very difficult." He had tried to remain calm but the agitation in his voice was very evident.

"Okay, meet me at the normal place in an hour." Her curt instruction gave no indication of flexibility so he turned the car around and headed for the coast.

CHAPTER 21

Julia Bare had accepted the job offer despite her husband's alternate viewpoint. She had concluded it was very early days in her pregnancy and it was important to carry on as normal. She had even kidded herself that her new employment might suit her so much that she would adopt the main breadwinner role and Bare could become a stay-at-home dad. She smiled as she recalled his face from the previous evening when she had muted the suggestion. His attempts to articulate a considered response without the risk of upsetting her had only caused her to prolong the fatuous suggestion, so much so that he had left for work earlier that morning wearing the same worried expression. She would let him swim in uncertainty for a little while longer before throwing him a lifebelt, she had decided. As a result of the relatively early stage of the pregnancy and their history the pair had vowed to keep it a secret for now so she resisted the strong temptation to share the news with her friend at their coffee date in town. Instead the women spoke about the new job and she listened as her friend told her that it was clearly the reason she had regained her 'glow'.

After the pair had parted Julia decided to buy a sandwich from the patisserie and drop it into the police station as a surprise lunch for 'Daddy Bare', the nickname she had bestowed on him the previous evening. She had avoided the building since leaving the police but remained familiar enough with its geography to stride in and wait patiently for the station clerk to admit her to the restricted front counter area.

She was immediately recognised by the smiling clerk who opened the door and gave her a warm embrace. After the normal 'catch-up' chat she was granted access to the operational side of the building. Despite the heightened terrorist security alert the station clerk had laughed at the suggestion she might require a security pass and had merely sought confirmation she remembered the way to her husband's office. As she walked along the corridors of the memory-laden building she wondered if some of the personnel that passed her had even realised she had ever worked there. She recalled her father had described his own departure from the service as like someone throwing a stone in a big lake. The ripples of memory quickly fade and then it's like you had never been there at all, he had said with a melancholy in his voice that she had not fully understood at the time.

"Julia, we must stop meeting like this," said Avery, dismissing the interaction with a junior colleague in favour of Mrs Bare.

Her awkwardness grew as Avery leaned forward to kiss her in the presence of the seemingly embarrassed staff member she vaguely recognised as being a Detective on her husband's team.

"Is that for me?" asked the undeterred Avery, pointing toward the sandwich she was now holding in both hands almost as a barrier to any further physical contact.

She smiled at the weak joke before unnecessarily explaining it was for her husband.

"Ah, story of my life," said Avery with theatrical disappointment before insisting on escorting her to DS Bare's office. The journey was mercifully short as Avery had continued his performance of suitor by linking their arms as they walked along the corridor.

"Does he know you are coming or are you hoping to catch him out with my secretary?" he asked in a loud voice as they arrived at Bare's open door.

Bare looked up and smiled at the unexpected presence of his wife and at the same time casually covered the Racing Times he had been studying with a nearby copy of the Police Gazette when he noted in whose company she was.

"You two clearly enjoy your lunches together, I shall leave you to it, nice seeing you again Julia," said Avery before departing with a smile that Julia later described as belonging to a 'sanctimonious wanker'. The description nearly made Bare choke with laughter as he continued eating the delicious sandwich.

CHAPTER 22

As a venue for a confidential meeting the partially renovated beachfront property was ideal. The owner, Mary Mackenzie, parked her car at the side and used the main entrance. Her visitor parked in the small parking area that served the nearby national heritage park and once satisfied nobody was in the area slipped through the gap in the fence which led to the rear door of the property. He opened the unlocked door and was at least relieved to see it was indeed Mary waiting for him rather than either of her sons. For a woman in her early sixties she looked good, dressed sharply in a black top and matching skirt. Her legs were accentuated by the high heels she was wearing which he correctly assumed to be of a designer brand.

"So nice of you to come, Jim, I have just made a coffee, would you like one?" she enquired.

Morton politely declined the offer; taking anything from the McKenzie family, even after all this time, felt uncomfortable.

"So let me get straight to the point so there are no misunderstandings. Stuart and I had no secrets as far as the business was concerned so I have been aware of your friendship with him from the start but I can reassure you that nobody else knows," she lied.

"Well obviously that's difficult for me to believe," replied Morton although he desperately hoped it to be true.

"It's in nobody's interest for our friendship to be divulged," she continued and Morton felt like he was talking with a reincarnation of her late husband. "But as Stuart would have told you our business is complicated."

"I don't need the full lecture," interjected Morton, surprised at the conviction in his own voice.

"Indeed, well I was just trying to reassure you that I see no reason why our infrequent contacts can't carrying on being mutually beneficial," she said, unperturbed by his interruption.

"I have an alternative proposition," said Morton, hoping that his hastily conceived plan would gain some traction in his new 'handler's' mind. "The new boss has commissioned an operation specifically targeting your family, if it turns up nothing then they won't carry on flogging a dead horse and provided you keep under the radar you will have free reign to continue."

"Go on," said Mary, sipping her coffee and listening intently.

"Okay, I can sabotage the operation and make it fail but I need you to suspend everything for three months. I will give you the all-clear once I know it's ended, but after that, it's over, I'm done, no more contact ever."

Morton looked at the woman seeking a 'tell' as to whether his proposal would be enough to secure his release from the unsigned contract he had entered into all those years before.

"Three months would be difficult, Jim, and very expensive. Could we say two?"

Morton's heart leapt at the fact she appeared willing to negotiate. "Well two is possible, it depends on how patient the boss is and I think he wants a quick result so yes, say two months."

"I can see a lot of logic in what you are saying, Jim, we could even throw you a bone or two to divert the dogs elsewhere so your boss gets his result," she added.

This was going better than Morton had envisaged; not only could he be discharged from work for the McKenzies but he could emerge as the saviour in Avery's eyes. "We have some loose intelligence surrounding an Albanian crime group with Manchester connections," he confided.

"Yes, we have had a couple of run-ins, I know Stuart was concerned, I am sure we could probably give you a hand with that," enthused Mary.

"Okay, do we have a deal?" said Morton, extending his hand by way of hopeful confirmation.

Instead of shaking his hand Mary put the tip of her own index finger in her mouth, an involuntary action when she was concentrating.

Morton waited, recognising she was seriously considering the matter.

"Who is running the operation against us?" she asked.

It was the subject Morton had been hoping to avoid had he suddenly doubted his proposal would be accepted.

"It's Sebastian Bare," he said wearily.

Mary McKenzie laughed out loud. "Well of course it is," she exclaimed whilst simultaneously shaking her head. "That man really doesn't like us, does he?"

Morton remained silent at the rhetorical question wondering how he could mitigate Bare's involvement.

"Can he be bought off?" she eventually asked flatly, clearly not expecting an affirmative answer.

"Bare is a bit of a complex character," said Morton. "He does tend to get obsessed with things but I think if he doesn't turn anything up he might lose interest and he certainly won't have any backing."

He saw from her facial expression that his platitude had not really satisfied Mary's question.

"Okay, tell me everything about him, tell me about his wife, where they live, what his vulnerabilities are," she said.

"No, I don't feel I can do that, he is my friend," said Morton, his head now bowed reflecting how dispirited he was feeling.

"Well then you will be doing your friend a favour by making sure the operation fails," said Mary with a comforting touch of Morton's shoulder. "But I need that information just as an insurance policy," she added.

Morton left the property thirty minutes later, the envelope containing two thousand pounds weighing heavily in his pocket as it always did. As he approached his car he noted the dark skies above and he heard the rumble of distant thunder.

CHAPTER 23

Avery had always found sex to be an unsatisfying and largely empty experience. It had taken him two hours to drive the hire vehicle to the red light area of the town he had carefully chosen and he was wondering if it had been worth the effort. Even though the vehicle was now displaying cloned registration plates he didn't want to risk another circuit of the dark streets. If anybody wanted to check his whereabouts via cell site analysis of his phone, not that they ever would, it would show him diligently working late in his office on the otherwise deserted top floor of the police station. Cleverly if anybody rang the number, not that anybody would as he wasn't on call, his phone would divert to the untraceable one in his pocket.

Just as he was reconciling himself to the fact that his thrill for the night would have to be derived solely from the well-executed preparatory stage of the crime, he saw her. She was wearing the traditional uniform of a street walker, low-cut top, short leather skirt and thigh-length boots. Her peroxide blonde hair and harsh make up masked her age but he would have guessed early twenties.

He stopped the car twenty feet ahead of her, enjoying her panic in the rear-view mirror as she struggled to quicken her pace for fear of missing a punter. When alongside the car she leaned down through the already open passenger window and asked him if he was 'looking for business'. He replied that he was and she quickly got into the car. Satisfied that the encounter had not been witnessed he began to drive off.

She began to recite her in-car menu of services, adding £10 to each one on the basis he looked affluent and had not asked her a price when she had first approached him. He ignored her and just pointed to the central console in the car where there was a large wad of notes secured by a rubber band. She took the cue and picked up the money, guessing it amounted to at least ten times her normal rate.

"Fuck," she said with a broad smile. "What do you want me to do for all this, darling?"

"Can I have your phone?" he asked.

With her mind still focused on a bumper pay day she instinctively produced her phone from somewhere within her top.

"Why do you want my phone?" she asked suspiciously.

"I lost mine and need one, I'll give you £500 for it," he said after a cursory visual inspection of it.

"Done," she replied, this was already easily her most profitable night of the year.

As instructed she dutifully turned off the phone and placed it in the glovebox of the car. "Do you know a quiet place to go, hun?" she asked whilst her hand seductively stroked his leg.

"Yes, just down here," he replied as the car turned into the unmarked road at the edge of the forest she recognised as a familiar location favoured by previous punters.

The robotic act of intercourse lasted only a couple of minutes before he withdrew and carefully removed the condom. The act had taken place with him standing behind her as she bent over the bonnet of his car. Her handprints were very evident on the polished metal but Avery didn't care as he knew he would thoroughly clean it inside and out before returning it. The last thing she said before he strangled her with his belt was how good a lover he was; he kind of liked that even though he knew it was a lie.

The deep grave in the forest had taken Avery a full day to prepare when he had visited the site two days earlier. He was gratified the camouflage was still in place indicating nobody had stumbled upon his preparation. He had removed all her clothes as they sometimes interfered with the speed of decomposition of a body. They would later be burnt along with the small number of personal effects he had taken from her small handbag. He made a mental note to spend his reclaimed cash quickly as he didn't want to be in possession of anything with her fingerprints or DNA on it. Avery had never fully understood why so-called intelligent serial killers collected trophies from their victims, it seemed a ridiculous notion for anyone interested in preserving their liberty.

He anticipated that by the morning she might be reported as a missing person but was confident that as he poured the chemical solution over her body to wash away any lingering trace evidence that nobody would find her final resting place. As he eventually walked back to the car he stopped to regain his breath. The exertion of the burial and final touches at the deposition site had been far greater than the actual murder. He took a moment to inhale the night air and was already feeling disappointed how transient the adrenaline rush of the whole episode had been. Previously his appetite would have been satisfied for months but he was already feeling hungry and clearly junk food was not going to provide him with the sustenance he needed.

As he drove back toward the bright lights of the city he reflected on the other notable aspect of his activity that night. Normally he would now be reliving the actual 'kill' in his mind, that intoxicating moment when he extinguished the light from somebody's eyes, but tonight had been different. It had taken him by surprise that the mental image he had needed to climax was the smiling face of Julia Bare.

CHAPTER 24

Operation Spider was not going well and Bare was struggling to hide his irritation. In many ways his unofficial operation that had preceded it had been a lot easier. Certainly there had been less bureaucracy and no bosses breathing down his neck to provide updates. His intelligence sources were only providing generic updates but were crucially lacking specific detail. He had gone out on a limb and promised Avery that bringing in a surveillance team from another Force would definitely yield results but if anything it had only served to demonstrate how much time the McKenzies appeared to be devoting to their legitimate enterprises. There had been some initial excitement with the identification of a previously unknown lock-up that was visited most days by one of the McKenzie boys but it had turned out to be where they received and stored imported alcohol before it was distributed further afield including to their own nightclub. A check with HMRC had even shown they were paying all the appropriate duty. Bare had asked for the surveillance to be extended but had not been surprised when Avery declined the request having expended 42k from the Constabulary coffers already for the unproductive week.

Bare wondered whether the McKenzies' criminality had evolved so much that the family members were able to never dirty their hands. After all, Stuart had been a pillar of society and his death had been much mourned locally much to the continued annoyance of Bare. He snapped himself out of that train of thought when DC Perkins made virtually the same suggestion.

"They are not the bloody Mafia, just a bunch of half-wit jocks who are taking the piss," he heard himself say.

"Yes Sarge," had been the only reply as Perkins took refuge in the pile of unprocessed intelligence reports on his desk, instantly regretting the vocalisation of his thoughts.

Avery's entrance into the office signalled a now daily unwelcome intrusion for Bare.

"How's it going?" asked the senior officer, knowing full well that had there been any significant development Bare would have instigated the contact himself.

"We are getting there slowly," replied Bare.

Avery didn't seek any elaboration and appeared engrossed in the pictorial criminal association chart displayed on the office wall. Perkins looked up nervously, expecting a critique of his artwork but none was forthcoming.

"I suppose Operation Spider is an apt name given the web of deceit you are attempting to unravel," offered Avery.

"I was thinking about Robert the Bruce when it got assigned," replied Perkins who at once reddened at the realisation Avery's comment had not been aimed at him.

"How do you mean?" asked Avery.

Perkins took an audible gulp. "Well Robert the Bruce took inspiration from the persistence of a climbing spider he was watching when he was hiding in a cave."

"And then the Scottish king emerged and slaughtered all his enemies," added Avery before concluding his brief visit.

"Oh well done," said Bare to his young assistant who could only offer an apologetic shrug in response.

CHAPTER 25

Avery came off the phone and had a rare moment of self-doubt. The Metropolitan Police was a massive organisation meaning he chose when to enjoy the limelight and when to remain in the shadows. Additionally there had been a plethora of resources to draw upon and a huge number of fish to shoot as they struggled to find room in the barrel. Now by way of stark contrast the one-time president of his fan club had just chastised him for spending the majority of his annual budget in two months without producing any tangible results. Platitudes of 'significant progress' and 'really promising intelligence' were no longer music to the ACC's ears and it was clear that the Chief Officers were beginning to doubt the ability of 'the special one'.

The solution was obvious to him and it didn't involve waiting for Bare to rediscover his mojo. He drove back to the house he had been renting since his return from London and parked on the driveway. Normally this is where it would be left, but on this occasion it was a temporary stop as he opened the garage door before returning to the vehicle and manoeuvring it inside. He then closed the garage door and entered the house via the interior door that connected it to the garage.

Once inside he checked his watch; the town centre traffic had delayed his journey but he still had ample time to retrieve the items he needed from the hiding place he had constructed in the loft. A few minutes later he checked his appearance in the full-length bedroom mirror. He had entered the house as a suited Detective Superintendent and now he was a uniformed Metropolitan Police officer. Despite the uniform being collected at different stages of his career the collective ensemble worked together perfectly. The belt exclusively used by officers carrying a firearm was the last item he put on. The gun itself was the only non-police-issue item of equipment. He had managed to acquire it whilst working as an exhibits officer during a raid in London several years earlier. His sleight of hand had also extended to six rounds of ammunition but only three now remained due to his practice session in Epping Forest. *Three rounds ought to be fine,* he thought as he carefully loaded the revolver and holstered it, still slightly irritated that it was not a perfect fit in the belt specifically designed for the sidearms carried by police. He had a choice of uniform headwear in his collection but went for the dark blue baseball cap used by armed officers. The cap fitted neatly in the pocket of his three-quarter-length 'civvy coat' that hid the uniform underneath. Then it was just a case of remembering the cable ties and sharp bladed combat knife for the first part of his mission. For the second part he packed the other items in a separate bag, adding to the change of clothes he had already prepared. Finally he opened the boot of the car and gauged how much petrol was in the two plastic green containers. After lifting them individually he was satisfied that he had enough so he opened the garage door and reversed the earlier entry procedure.

Taking his own car meant he couldn't drive into the remote industrial estate, but the surveillance team had already identified the perfect vantage point from where to observe the lock-up. Consequently he turned down the track leading to the nature reserve and parked his vehicle in one of the many forest trails. It was now

5.30pm and already starting to get dark, the chilly winter evening very evident as soon as he turned off the car engine. He waited a minute for his eyes to adjust to the darkness and adjusted his interior light so there was no sudden artificial illumination as he got out of the vehicle. Even in the unlikely event someone else elected to drive down the track he was confident the chances of them spotting his vehicle were minuscule. Whilst the location was perfect in that aspect, it did mean a hazardous ten-minute walk down a foliage-covered steep hill before he reached the rear of the lock-up. Crouching behind the bushes he placed the petrol cans down on the ground and covered them with his jacket. He put the baseball cap on and was once again transformed into an armed police officer.

He had a clear view of all four lock-ups that now occupied what the surveillance team had discovered to be on the edge of an old airfield. He was gratified that none of the single-storey units had any lights on, corroborating the research that only one of the others aside from the target property was in use. The surveillance photographs he had viewed had helpfully labelled the other unit as belonging to a semi-retired furniture restorer who only used his unit until lunchtime each day. Another check of his watch revealed it to be 5.50pm and the cold weather intensified his hope that the McKenzie brothers were creatures of habit.

After half an hour passed he was on the verge of giving up when the bright headlights illuminated the front of the building. He had lowered himself so that he was completely behind some bushes to avoid any possibility of detection. Only when the car parked did he adjust his position slightly to see who had arrived. It appeared to be the white BMW that was habitually driven by Sean but when the occupants alighted he could see it was a male and female couple now standing at the front of the lock-up. After a few seconds' intense scrutiny he was fairly confident it was actually the older brother Liam and possibly his wife Shannon. His identification was confirmed as he overheard some brief dialogue between the pair that included the wife's name being used by her husband.

Now he had a decision to make, he had rehearsed the scene multiple times in his mind but it had only ever involved either of the brothers attending alone. The presence of a third party complicated matters and certainly added to the risk. But Avery's supreme confidence in his own ability told him it was safe to proceed and he readied himself for them to unlock the door and deactivate the alarm.

He was now close enough to hear the alarm code being entered by Liam; annoyingly Shannon had walked past her husband into the building before he had completed the task. Avery froze as he heard Liam loudly use an expletive and then realised it related to a mistaken code entry. Avery waited for the correct code to be entered and this time heard the prolonged audible confirmation tone from the alarm control pad. This was his cue to run forward with the firearm held outstretched in a two-hand grip.

"Armed police, stay where you are."

The shouted command had an instant effect on Liam who after a brief turn to see the approaching police officer raised both hands in surrender. Shannon rapidly appeared at the open doorway and took longer to comprehend the second shouted instruction but within a few moments was lying face-down on the cold gravel alongside her husband. Complying with another shouted instruction to look away from the police officer she heard her husband being handcuffed before her own wrists were secured behind her back with what felt like a cable tie.

CHAPTER 26

Bare's mood was not improved by the volume of traffic he had encountered on the way to London. Avery had arranged for him to meet a financial analyst who had been tasked with the forensic examination of the McKenzies' accounts and he was running late for their scheduled early evening appointment. Normally he would have looked forward to an overnight stay in the capital but the prospect of spending the evening alongside some nerd discussing things he was unlikely to ·understand had curbed his enthusiasm. He consoled himself with the fact that at least Avery had not pulled the plug on Operation Spider and by engaging the services of his Met contact was at least showing some support.

After checking into the pre-booked hotel, an establishment undeserving of its two stars that were proudly displayed next to its half-illuminated name, Bare rang Julia. He had offered to take her on the short trip but the prospect of Christmas shopping alone whilst her husband was tied up in meetings had limited appeal. Instead she had instructed him to make a reservation at the hotel for the following weekend so they could both enjoy spending his money in Oxford Street and maybe take in a West End show. Bare was not overly keen on the idea as he had a better understanding of the couple's finances due to a number of recent unsuccessful 'investments' with local bookmakers. He was gratified that his accurate description of the hotel's ambience seemed to be enough to put her off the proposal but the call worryingly ended with her vowing to look for a better place online.

As Bare waited for the analyst to arrive at the restaurant he wondered if his time as a detective was coming to an end. If criminals could only be brought to justice by someone armed with a calculator and a degree in accountancy, what did the future hold for him? Perhaps Avery was a personification of the future, operating at a cerebral level and scorning the grunts who kicked doors in and slapped the cuffs on. As he morosely swilled the remaining scotch in his glass he noticed the strikingly attractive woman smiling as she strode confidently toward him.

"So sorry I am late, you must be DS Bare?" she said, offering him a perfectly manicured hand to shake.

"And you must be Robin," replied Bare, belatedly realising the name was gender neutral.

The pair enjoyed a relaxed dinner and Bare provided an overview of the McKenzie family. Robin, whilst freely admitting to be the nerd he had been anticipating, stated that it helped her decipher the figures if she had some understanding of the crime family dynamics. Bare spoke freely and answered all of the questions she asked, enjoying her wide-eyed appreciation when recalling the arrest of the young McKenzie robbers. His instruction from Avery to 'wine and dine' the young analyst as a show of appreciation for their work now seemed a lot less onerous than when he had received it. He was only restrained when initially talking about his boss with Robin as he was unsure of her relationship with him. Perhaps sensing this, she immediately put his mind to rest with a humorous character assassination of her departed supervisor and laughed out loud when Bare confided how the nickname he had attributed to Avery had been so cruelly corrupted by colleagues.

At the end of the evening to the surprise of both of them and particularly Bare, there was no invitation back to his hotel room for a night cap. Experience had told him that any such invitation would have been readily accepted but at the point of offering it he had stopped himself and the pair parted with a mutual acknowledgement of their 9am coffee date the following morning. As he made the solo walk back to his hotel Bare wondered in how many other ways the arrival of a child would change his life.

CHAPTER 27

The initial submissive compliance at the sight of the firearm had now subsided and been replaced by indignation. Liam McKenzie was now, like his wife, secured by cable ties around his hands and ankles. She had been afforded the luxury of being restrained while sitting on the one chair in the lock-up whilst he was on the floor opposite her. The police officer had told them it was necessary for them to be restrained whilst he waited for his 'backup' to arrive.

None of this was making any sense to Liam who was confident that he had followed his mother's instructions to the letter and had not even committed the offence of littering in the last two months. Also despite his repeated demands the strangely behaving cop had not told them the reason for their arrest or offered any of the rights he was fairly certain they were entitled to. Shannon's persistent crying was not helping him focus either and he was regretting his last-minute decision to invite her along to break the monotony of the tasks his mother had given him. There was something else strange about the cop that was niggling McKenzie. He had stated he was waiting for others to arrive but not once had Liam heard him converse with others on his radio or phone.

After making a check that no one else was in the lock-up Avery returned to his prisoners. His earlier cursory search of both had yielded both their phones and the bunch of keys that he was now holding in his hands. Avery dangled the keys in front of Liam and broke his silence with a strange question.

"Why have you got Sean's car?"

Liam considered the question and jumped to the conclusion that his brother had been the intended target of the police operation.

"Have you arrested the wrong brother, occifer?" he mocked. "Cause we have just dropped him in town for a drink." He was being partly truthful in that Sean had been due to visit the lock-up that evening but had begged a favour of his brother to replace him. Sean had not been coping with the parameters set by their mother and wanted to socialise unsupervised. Liam had agreed to be his substitute and had indeed dropped him off at a pub en route. They had taken Sean's car in case Mary had checked that her schedule was being adhered to. Liam made a mental note to kick his brother's arse for whatever else he had done to warrant an armed arrest.

Seemingly satisfied with the explanation offered by McKenzie, Avery then continued his odd behaviour by producing a Dictaphone from his pocket.

"Okay, we don't have much time," said Avery whilst switching the device on to record mode. "I need to know everything about how your family operates, so let's start with where and how you import drugs."

"Fuck off, our solicitor is having you for breakfast, take us to the nick now," laughed McKenzie.

His humour at the outrageous question quickly subsided as he saw Avery casually tying a gag around his wide-eyed wife's mouth.

"What the fuck are you doing?" his own eyes now burning with rage.

"Answer the question or I will hurt Shannon," said Avery with a calm authority as he produced a larger combat knife from a thigh pocket.

"Fuck off, I'm going to—" His threat was incomplete as the knife suddenly was stabbed into his wife's left thigh and her muffled scream confirmed it was a genuine attack.

"You bastard!" screamed McKenzie, making a hopeless attempt to get to his feet. A double palm strike to his chest sent him down to the concrete floor and with no free hands to break his fall his face painfully impacted on the surface. Avery pulled him back into a seated position and McKenzie saw the knife remained in place in Shannon's leg as tears streamed down her terrified face.

"If I pull this knife out now there is a good chance her femoral artery will make her bleed to death, do you understand, Liam?" said Avery in the same assured tone.

McKenzie could only nod in response, the panic on his face mirroring his wife's.

"Good, now you were about to tell me about the drugs side of things," said Avery, turning the Dictaphone to face McKenzie to ensure the explanation was clearly recorded.

As Liam spoke his eyes were fixed on Shannon as Avery was carefully applying an impromptu tourniquet fashioned from her own neck scarf to her leg. If McKenzie paused or provided an explanation lacking the required detail he was prompted by Avery making a beckoning gesture with his fingers indicating the interrogator wanted more. Liam was astute enough to recognise the correlation between him speaking and his wife not being hurt further but his mind was already racing ahead to what would happen when his account was finished. After nearly an hour of providing enough detail to incriminate every family member he could think of, Liam had only one card left to play.

"Are you a real cop? I mean you can never use any of the stuff I have told you."

"Maybe not as evidence, but you have told me enough to bring your family down," Avery replied.

"There is something else, but before I say it you have to let Shannon go."

"Okay and if I don't?" asked Avery.

"Then you will never find out why we are always one step ahead of you," responded McKenzie, hoping that his power play would somehow lead to an end to the ordeal.

Avery gave a reassuringly warm smile.

"Okay son, here's your never to be repeated one-time offer, you tell me your little secret and I will walk away, it's up to you whether you tell Mummy what's happened or fuck off to Spain with whatever you've got stashed away for a rainy day. If you come after me I will not only kill you and your delightful wife but I will slowly slit the throat of young Cameron too."

Liam McKenzie knew that he was in no position to negotiate and despite everything clung to the hope he was dealing with a renegade cop rather than a murderer. He provided the name that appeared to genuinely shock his tormentor.

"Thank you, Liam," said Avery and he slowly withdrew his holstered revolver and shot McKenzie with total accuracy in the centre of his forehead. Shannon could only plead with her eyes as her gag remained in place whilst Avery slowly removed the knife from her thigh. His adjustment of the bandage position gave her some hope he was going to permit her to live but as he moved behind her she felt the cold steel at her neck and knew that her life was over.

Even though he was behind schedule Avery took a moment to savour the sight of his first murder scene involving two bodies. He wanted to stay longer but had much to do so he quickly plucked some hairs from Liam McKenzie's head and carefully placed them in a small plastic bag he had brought for that specific purpose. As he left the lock-up he put on a pair of disposable gloves before getting into the car parked outside. He was delighted that it contained the bonus of some cigarette stubs in the ashtray. He discarded one immediately as it had some lipstick on it but carefully packaged two others, not really caring which of the brothers had smoked them.

Fifteen minutes later he drove the BMW along the road adjacent to the apartment block he would later visit. The vehicle had no problem reaching the necessary speed and the bright flash in his rear-view mirror confirmed the speed camera was working. There were no other surveillance devices he had to worry about so he then drove sensibly back to the crime scene he had left thirty minutes earlier. This time before entering the building he retrieved the concealed petrol containers.

A quick check of the interior confirmed it was exactly as he had left it although both bodies were now beginning to show the grey pallor of death. He emptied the petrol liberally around the building although he knew it was rather superfluous given the boxes of stored alcohol there. One open box caught his eye and he removed a bottle of red wine from it. A quick examination of the label revealed it to be a Massolino Parussi Barolo 2015 and he put it to one side by the door after nodding appreciatively at Liam McKenzie's corpse.

Saving enough petrol for the interior of the BMW, Avery was

satisfied his work there was done. As he quickly made his way back to his own parked vehicle he looked back and saw the flames were already illuminating the night sky. Now he just needed another quick clothes change before his next appointment.

CHAPTER 28

It was nearly 11pm when he arrived at the front door of the top-floor apartment. Just one hour left before it was his birthday and he had no doubt it would be a memorable one. It was a calculated risk she would be at home and alone, but there again what else was there to do on a cold Tuesday night?

Julia looked at the text she had received from Bare and hoped it signalled he was retiring alone to his hotel bed. She was trying to formulate a reply in her mind when her thoughts were interrupted by the shrill sound of the doorbell. The sudden noise coupled with the totally unexpected late-night intrusion made her almost drop her phone. With some degree of composure regained she walked toward the door and wondered if this was to be an elaborate surprise from her husband having prematurely concluded his business in London. Instead the spy hole revealed Paul Avery to be waiting patiently outside. Her heartbeat accelerated again as the only reason senior officers traditionally made unannounced house calls was to deliver agony messages. She quickly reminded herself that she had only just received a text from her husband which indicated he was alive and well so opened the door displaying a puzzled expression.

"Hello Julia, so sorry to disturb you," said Avery.

"Err, Seb is in London," she replied, anticipating Avery was seeking her husband.

"Yes I know, it's you I need to speak to, it's a bit delicate, may I come in?"

"Oh yes, of course," she replied, embarrassed that she had not invited him in sooner.

Avery followed her along the short hallway and into the lounge; he was disappointed she was not wearing the night attire that he had imagined when previewing the encounter in his mind.

"Please have a seat," she said but made no move to sit down herself.

Avery removed his coat and placed it on the one available armchair along with the leather bag she saw he had been carrying. His choice of coat rack meant the large sofa was the only remaining place for him to sit and she instinctively sat at the other end.

"What is this about?" she asked, unwilling to wait any longer to understand the purpose of his late-night visit.

"It's about Seb, don't worry he's not hurt or anything like that," said Avery, "but it's important for you to know I am here as his friend first and boss second."

Julia's nod was not meant to show any understanding but just a need for Avery to continue with his explanation.

"I don't know if he has told you much about the operation he is working on?"

Julia struggled to understand the relevance of the question but answered it in the hope it would expedite her comprehension.

"Well I know it's about the McKenzie family," she stated, unsure whether she ought to be betraying her husband's breach of confidentiality to a senior officer.

"Yes, and I think we both know it's something he is very personally invested in."

She again nodded in response, knowing that fact was probably an open secret, waiting for Avery's concern to be articulated.

"Look, I think Seb is in real danger of crossing the line and could land himself in serious trouble, I think a lot of him but don't think he listens to a word I say so I wondered if we could come up with a plan to save him from himself."

"Oh, is that it?" said a relieved Julia. "I thought you were going to tell me he had done something terrible like beat one of them up or something, my heart is thumping, I think I need a drink."

"Well that's what I want to avoid before it all goes horribly wrong and as for the drink, why don't you try a glass of this little beauty I have just acquired?" said Avery, reaching for the bottle of red wine from his bag.

As Julia fetched two glasses from the kitchen she justified her imminent alcohol consumption by weighing it up against the stress Bare was causing her with whatever stupid thing he was about to do or knowing him, had already done. The last thing she needed right know was to have to keep his creepy boss onside. At least she would have a bloody good excuse to ring him once she had ushered Avery out of the door and he had bloody well better be alone, she concluded.

She turned around and was startled to find Avery standing there with the now open wine bottle in his hand.

"Allow me to pour," he said and in response she put the glasses down on the work surface. The tiny kitchen in their modern apartment meant the occupancy of two people was always an intimate affair. Unwilling to prolong the experience she immediately excused herself to visit the bathroom. As she edged past him she sensed his lack of movement meant he was enjoying the brief physical contact and she mouthed a silent, "Fuck," as she entered the bathroom and locked the door. Sitting on the toilet she wondered how much of Avery's visit was a genuine offer of assistance and how much was going to be a clumsy attempt to seduce her. Her ability to read men left her in no doubt that the latter option was far more likely. She would have to utilise all the 'f's, she decided as she formulated her strategy. Be friendly, firm and if all else fails tell him to fuck off.

Avery had also read the body language on display and had sadly concluded the conquest he had planned would fail unless he had some assistance. Luckily the Rohypnol he had mixed into her full wine glass was likely to be a strong ally. The so-called 'date-rape' drug typically took fifteen minutes to work and its sedative effect was at least ten times stronger than Valium. Its odourless quality and invisibility when mixed in a dark drink had made it a perfect companion for countless rapists over the years particularly as residual side effects often included total or partial memory loss by the victim.

When a resolute Julia reappeared she was pleasantly surprised that Avery did not appear the least flirtatious as he slowly explained his specific areas of concern that could lead to a collapse of Operation Spider and a custodial sentence for her husband. She wondered whether the Detective Superintendent was just odd and she had misread the signals. Nevertheless she quickly drank the large glass of very nice wine he had given her so as to hasten his exit. Her last conscious memory was him carrying her to the bedroom and her being powerless to resist.

Once Avery had carefully stripped Julia naked he placed all the clothes she had been wearing in the wicker laundry basket. He was fascinated to observe the effects of the drug she had involuntarily ingested. Occasionally her eyes would open and there had even been some slurred speech as he explored her body with his fingertips. He had not raped her after concluding the reality could never compete with the fantasy, but had enjoyed the intimate examination of her body.

He left her briefly and opened the door that led to the balcony. It was smaller than he had imagined but he was reassured that the design of the apartment block meant it was not overlooked. The balcony itself was bordered by waist-high safety glass so if you were sitting there on a balmy evening, sipping a wine you could view the busy world below without peering over the edge. At 4am in the November morning it was far from balmy as he returned to the bedroom and saw Julia appeared to be sleeping soundly. It was difficult to dress her in the black silk pyjamas that she had conveniently left on her pillow for him but he eventually managed it. He carried her back into the lounge and this time left her on the floor by the balcony door before returning to the bedroom for a final time. He was delighted to find the unopened box of anti-depressant tablets in the en-suite medicine cabinet. Inspection of the label suggested they had been prescribed to Julia a couple of months previously and he wondered why they remained intact. He completed his staged scene with the placement of a couple of Liam McKenzie's hairs in the Bares' bed.

Avery then returned to the lounge and managed to rouse Julia enough to feed her the contents of her prescription, washing down the medicine with the remains of the wine they had enjoyed earlier. There was no fear in her eyes as he took her onto the balcony, lifting her to sit on the guard rail and face inwards. He of course had to support her with his arms around her waist meaning hers naturally went over his shoulders like lovers enjoying an embrace. Then he was alone on the balcony in total silence as Julia fell to her death without even a whimper of complaint.

CHAPTER 29

The junior officer who had collected Avery from his office was full of apologies for not knowing the answers to his Detective Superintendent's questions. It had been a manic start to the day with the Fire Brigade now reporting they had discovered two bodies at the lock-up connected to the McKenzies and uniform colleagues trying to identify a dead female found in a bloody heap on a pavement in town.

"We've got the Major Investigation Team at the fire and uniform officers at the apparent suicide," explained the escorting officer.

"Okay, we need Operation Spider staff involved in the fire, get hold of DS Bare and ask him to get back from London as soon as possible," instructed Avery, "and where is DI Morton?" he added as an apparent afterthought.

"I think he is day off today, sir."

"Okay, let's go see the dead woman," sighed Avery.

Upon entering the area of road cordoned off by blue and white chequered tape Avery resisted the temptation to immediately look up at the top-floor balcony where he had been standing less than four hours earlier. The Detectives had been beaten to the scene by a uniformed sergeant anxious to ensure her staff had done the basics correctly. She had only needed a brief view of the body to recognise it as being that of a friend and former colleague. Avery had to feign a puzzled expression as the Sergeant hurriedly walked towards him with tears already evident in her eyes.

"Sir, it's Julia Bare," her trembling voice managed to convey.

"What do you mean?" he replied, prolonging the theatre.

The Sergeant was forced to deliver the agony message a second time and immediately realised that Avery's shocked reaction meant he also had known the former officer.

"I think her and Seb live here," she added and pointed to the adjacent block for additional clarification.

"Oh I see," said Avery, allowing himself to slowly look up at the complex. "Do you happen to know which apartment, Sergeant?"

The Detective Superintendent took two uniformed officers with him to the top-floor apartment. He had informed the relieved Sergeant that she would not have to break the news to Sebastian Bare who was believed to be en route from London having been recalled in respect of Operation Spider. Avery had requested that a further message be relayed telling the unsuspecting officer to come straight to his office upon his return with no deviations.

When they arrived at the apartment door the constables looked to their senior officer for guidance. Avery stepped forward and knocked loudly on the door. To the astonishment of all three, the door was immediately opened by a woman who mirrored their expressions with an equally perplexed face. The situation became more complicated by the fact that it soon became obvious English was not her first language. Avery looked beyond her into the hallway and having seen the vacuum cleaner plugged in ready for use was the first to solve the puzzle as to her role.

"Are you Mr and Mrs Bare's cleaner?" he asked slowly in the manner of an English tourist abroad.

"Yes but they not home," came the reply which at least indicated a degree of comprehension.

Leaving the more junior of the two constables to explain their presence Avery motioned for the other officer to follow him around the apartment. As they passed the bedroom a cursory glance was enough to tell him his crime scene had not yet been cleaned. The fresh smell of furniture polish in the lounge together with a closed balcony door did however indicate the cleaner had been industrious in that area.

As Avery visually surveyed the scene the other officer joined them from the hallway with some hastily written notes in his notebook.

"Maria Hernandez is the cleaner, she has been here about 30 mins, thinks the Bares must have gone out early so just cracked on with the cleaning, didn't notice anything unusual, sir," was the officer's succinct report.

"Has she been out there?" asked Avery, pointing toward the balcony.

"Err, I will just go check, sir, she didn't mention it."

Avery was about to list other questions he wanted the officer to ask the woman when he was distracted by the other officer opening the balcony door at the same time as a noise from the hallway indicated a resumption of vacuum cleaning.

"Oh for fuck's sake, come away from there, it's a potential crime scene," snapped Avery, "and tell her to switch that bloody thing off."

After locking down the scene Avery returned to the ground floor, delegating containment command to the Sergeant.

"I know Julia had been very depressed after leaving the job but I never thought she would do this," said the Sergeant.

"You and your officers need to stop jumping to bloody conclusions, the very least Julia deserves is for her former colleagues to investigate this properly, I want a full forensic on that apartment," ordered Avery. "Now can I trust you to do your jobs while I go and break the news to her poor sod of a husband?" he added, enjoying his occupancy of the moral high ground.

"Yes sir, sorry sir, of course you are right," she replied, embarrassed by her lack of professionalism.

Avery's tone immediately softened and he gave her a reassuring pat on the arm.

"Sorry, I didn't mean to snap, it's just not the way I envisaged I would spend my birthday."

He then turned away and walked toward the waiting police car, thrilled that this was turning out to be another momentous birthday.

CHAPTER 30

The sudden silence that engulfed the main CID office indicated to Bare he had missed something of consequence. He had not adhered to the instruction to go straight to the Headmaster's office as his 'forewarned is forearmed' mantra was deeply ingrained and had previously served him well. The silence was broken by the surreal entrance of Jim Morton wearing the most garish golf outfit imaginable.

"I got here as quick as I could, mate," said Morton in a breathless voice highlighting he had chosen stairs over the unreliable lift.

"Guv'nor, he's only just got here," said a junior colleague, relieved that the burden of responsibility had clearly passed to the higher rank now in the room.

"Oh Christ," said Morton, quickly assessing the unfolding scene. "Come with me."

The pair walked to Morton's office with Bare struggling to keep up with his friend's unusually brisk pace. Once inside with the door closed for privacy Bare didn't wait for the inevitable accusation to be levelled at him.

"Before you say anything I was in London all last night so whoever torched their place it was nothing to do with me."

Morton had not yet been briefed about the McKenzie fire and had only left the golf course following a call from a Sergeant at the scenes of Julia Bare's death.

"Seb, I have no idea what you are talking about but I am so sorry."

His explanation was left incomplete as Avery walked into the office having been alerted to the fact that Bare was in the building. The confused expression on the Detective Sergeant's face indicated that nobody had yet broken the news to him.

"Do you want me to go, sir?" offered an apologetic Morton.

"Oh will somebody just tell me what I am supposed to have done now?" interrupted an increasingly frustrated Bare.

Avery proceeded to break the news in a calm, professional, yet incredibly compassionate way to the disbelieving widower. Bare sat with his head bowed struggling to comprehend the reason his early morning call to Julia had gone unanswered. Morton shifted uncomfortably in his seat, also listening attentively to Avery and desperately hoping the senior officer was describing his earlier attendance at a suicide.

Bare was in shock, a thousand questions entered his mind but then left before he could vocalise them. Avery was talking about support and making promises that he would find answers to any of his questions but all Bare wanted right now was to be somewhere else. He didn't know where he wanted to be but he knew it wasn't here and he knew he wanted to be alone. It took him a moment to stand up as it felt like his legs were going to betray him but he finally managed it and without explanation he left the office and went into the small toilet opposite. After bolting the door he just made it into the cubicle before he was violently sick in the bowl. He remained slumped in the cubicle until the nausea finally passed and then took the opportunity to splash cold water over his face whilst staring at the mirror above the sink.

When he emerged he saw Avery and Morton were patiently waiting for him and there were now three cups of fresh coffee on Morton's desk. As he sipped the coffee he listened again as Avery repeated the information he had already provided to ensure Bare had a full understanding. There might have been times in the past when after hearing the explanation of the scene that Bare would have concluded suicide was the likely cause of his wife's death. Bare confirmed his wife had previously taken anti-depressants and conceded that she had a borderline alcohol problem but was adamant that she would not have taken her own life. When the other two looked at him quizzically as to why he could be so certain, he realised he had not told them Julia was pregnant. After hearing himself say this Bare wept for the first time he could remember since his childhood.

CHAPTER 31

Routine made Morton sit at the breakfast table though he had no appetite after a restless night. His arrival in the kitchen was barely acknowledged by Stephanie who was engrossed in some tabloid article. The empty coffee jug did little to improve Morton's mood particularly when it was obvious that his wife had refreshed her own cup moments earlier. Instead, he sipped a glass of fresh orange juice. Ignoring the now cold slices of toast in a small metal rack he picked up the newspaper, half expecting his name to appear in the headlines. The 'night of terror' had happened earlier in the week but continued to occupy the front page. He took little solace from the absence of any personal reference but noted that the suspicious deaths associated with the McKenzie fire had taken precedence over the demise of Julia Bare.

"What time did you get in?" asked Stephanie, without looking up from the salacious detail of burnt bodies that dominated the pages in front of her.

"It was late," he replied whilst formulating a believable reason in his mind to address the supplementary question that was sure to follow.

Surprisingly, it didn't. Instead, Stephanie spoke about her plans for the day as if he were a Personal Assistant who was required to complete her important diary. Morton retreated into his own troubled world, occasionally surfacing to provide the minimum input required to sustain his wife's dialogue. He noted a few minutes later that she was silent, clearly anticipating something more than a nod or a muttered acknowledgement.

"I'm sorry, what did you say?" he said.

"I asked if there had been any developments in the death of poor Julia," she repeated, making little effort to disguise the annoyance in her voice.

"Um, no, not really, there are quite a few lines of enquiry though," he replied.

"Lines of enquiry? I'm supposed to be your wife, not some journalist. What the fuck does that mean?"

Morton was shocked at her outburst but correctly assumed it was merely a precursor to what had become a regular statement of discontent from his wife.

"You used to talk to me, Jim, but now I feel like a stranger to you. What's the matter with you?"

"I'm sorry," he mumbled. "I've got a lot on my mind. This has really affected the whole station. Nobody knows what to say to Bare and it's…" His voice dropped to inaudible, causing Stephanie to place her hand on his.

"No, I'm sorry," she said in softer tones. "It must be hard for you."

"It really is," he replied, feeling guilty that he had used the death to extricate himself from what had seemed an inevitable discussion about the state of their marriage.

"How is Bare coping?" she asked.

"Bare is... well, Bare. I have no idea what's going on inside his head half the time."

"Do you think he killed her?" Stephanie asked matter-of-factly.

"No of course not," rebuked Morton, irritated by his wife's lack of sensitivity but not surprised by it. "It looks like suicide."

"Well, some people must think that he did, I mean those that don't know him like you," said Stephanie.

"I guess so," said Morton, not wishing to prolong the discussion.

After Stephanie left for work, Morton was left alone to contemplate the day ahead. He was scheduled to work a late shift so there was no rush to do anything other than slump in his favourite armchair. His thoughts inevitably centred around his own position and he tried to play out all the different potential scenarios in his mind. With a weary resignation he looked at the caller display on his ringing phone and saw that once again it signalled an incoming request to speak from a withheld number. He terminated the call rather than let it ring out hoping in vain that she would take the hint and leave him alone.

CHAPTER 32

Mary McKenzie had experienced every type of emotion during the preceding 72 hours. It had started with hostility at the sight of a uniformed police officer at her door in the early hours, based on an assumption that it signalled a raid of her property. Her mood had changed to concern upon being told of the fire that was raging at the lock-up. When she had been told that a vehicle was also alight she had rushed outside and confirmed Sean's car was missing. A check of his room had revealed it to be empty and her panicking fingers struggled to summons his number on her phone. With the police officer waiting patiently for any information she listened to the ring tone, willing it to be answered. Relief flooded through her when she heard his intoxicated, slurred, wonderful voice struggling to communicate against the backdrop of a noisy nightclub. The relief morphed into confusion as he guiltily admitted that his older brother was in fact in possession of his car.

This time she had knocked on the bedroom door, not wishing to disturb a married couple in the same way she had been prepared to rouse Sean from his slumber. There had been no reply so she had entered and found the double bed to be empty. Instinctively she looked in the other annexe bedroom and was gratified at least that her grandson was sleeping soundly. As she walked back to the police officer still waiting patiently at her front door she rang both Liam and Shannon but could gain no reply from either.

The police officer was clearly receiving some additional information from the scene as his brow furrowed in concentration as he struggled to hear the radio transmission via his earpiece. Then the look that he gave her betrayed any confidence he had been asked to keep by his control room. She seized upon it, demanding to know what was going on, ignoring his platitudes for calm.

"The fire service are reporting they have recovered two bodies," he reluctantly informed her.

She had needed no further information, the intuition of a mother was rarely wrong in her experience. The young police officer had tried to interpret her cold stare but she had dismissed him with an instruction to return when he had more information. After closing the door she leaned against the hall wall for support before slumping to the ground in a flood of tears. She had remained in the position for nearly an hour until the taxi containing Sean arrived.

After the identities of her eldest son and daughter-in-law had been confirmed it had been a procession of detectives who had been confusingly supportive. Her family had never been treated as victims before and she did not know how to react, so she withdrew and concentrated on the one obvious and necessary task to comfort her grandson. It was only now that her anger had replaced all the other emotions that she had tried to contact Morton for an inside track on the investigation.

CHAPTER 33

Bare stared at the half-empty bottle of vodka and contemplated what the next few days would have in store. The world around him was playing at fast-forward and the alcohol before him represented the nearest thing to a pause button he could find. Even his relatively complex life up to yesterday now seemed incredibly straightforward in comparison to the present and foreseeable future. He had desperately tried to feel the grief that was touching others far less close to Julia that he had been, but in truth he couldn't. Nothing was penetrating the numbness that enveloped him. He wondered how long it would be before his colleagues knew how to receive his entry into a room and how many more premature silences he would cause by catching those people, engrossed in conversation, unawares.

Bare studied his colleagues as they passed him in the corridor, obviously shocked at his presence in the station. He had told the first to enquire the truth. He simply had nowhere else to go. No close family, no close friends and his home was still a 'scene'. Avery had encouraged him to stay at the hotel and Morton had invited him to occupy a spare room at his house but both had quickly acquiesced in the face of his abrupt rebuttals. His rationale was simple; the uncomfortable truth was that a suicide was much easier for the bosses than an expensive murder investigation. So whilst forensic test results were awaited he intended to be a very visual reminder that there was going to be no opportunity to take any shortcuts. Paradoxically of course he was aware that the major enquiry competing for the limited investigative resources was the double McKenzie murder, but that had failed to stir even the mildest interest in him.

The Detective Chief Inspector allocated the double murder investigation, Gareth Jones, hesitated before entering Bare's office. The two had never worked together but he had heard that the Detective Sergeant could be an awkward customer at the best of times and this clearly was not the best of times for Bare. Nevertheless, he and his team had a job to do and he was always going to need to speak to the officer in charge of Operation Spider.

"I realise that you are going through a terrible time but I wonder if you are up to a chat?"

Bare looked up and saw the Welsh harmonic tone belonged to DCI Jones and gestured to the empty chair opposite him. The experienced senior officer had a good reputation in the Constabulary and Bare felt duty bound to comply given the sincere approach that had been made. Almost despite himself Bare became intrigued as Jones provided a rapid brief of the murder investigation. He listened attentively as Jones confided that both Liam and Shannon had been killed before the fire had been set and the enquiry team's early hypothesis was this appeared to be a double execution. Without being asked Bare quickly provided names of crime groups that could be considered rivals of the McKenzies which Jones contemporaneously recorded in a virgin note book he had brought into the office. The distraction of recounting his history with the McKenzies seemed to allow Bare a brief moment of freedom from his own personal grief until Jones brought it back into sharp focus.

"And I understand you were in London actually speaking to a financial analyst about the family when it all happened?"

"Well at the time happened I was asleep in my hotel room," said Bare, instantly welling up as he again felt the guilt of his abstraction on that fateful night.

"Yes of course," replied Jones, silently cursing the insensitive framing of his own question. "I wonder, have you got the report from the analyst yet?"

Bare took a breath to regain his composure whilst logging onto his email account.

"I haven't checked but Robin said she would send it over," he explained whilst scanning the long list of unopened mail on his account. The Metropolitan Police tag made the email stand out and Bare pressed the button causing the nearby printer to come noisily to life.

Jones stood up and retrieved the long report and saw that Bare had also printed the accompanying short email. After quickly reading it he handed the single sheet to Bare whilst retaining the hard copy of the report.

"Well thanks for your time, and so sorry about your wife, I hope you get some answers," said Jones with a farewell handshake.

Bare sat back in his chair, genuinely impressed by the DCI which was a rarity for him in relation to senior officers. He then read the email from Robin and doubted whether he had given Gareth Jones the same positive impression.

'Hey handsome please find attached the promised report, shame you had to rush off as I was hoping for another dinner date and maybe.......xxxx"

Bare crumpled the paper into a ball and threw it the waste bin next to his desk.

CHAPTER 34

The urgent meeting between Avery and DCI Jones had been hastily convened following receipt of the forensic results. He had listened carefully and shown appropriate shock at the revelation that Liam McKenzie had at some stage been in Julia Bare's bed. Not only that but a cigarette probably extinguished in the earth of a plant pot on the Bares' balcony had also yielded a full DNA profile.

"Also Liam McKenzie?" asked Avery in the most incredulous voice he could muster.

"Nope, that one belongs to Sean McKenzie," said Jones.

"Bloody hell, so they were both there?" said Avery, shaking his head in disbelief.

"There's more, guv'nor," said Jones, enjoying the theatre of his revelations. "A wine bottle was retrieved from the kitchen bin; it's been wiped clean but a print belonging to Liam McKenzie was still found on the base and Julia's DNA is around the top."

"Wow, good work Gareth," said Avery whilst remembering how carefully he had to handle the bottle once he had pressed Liam's dead fingers onto the base.

"It's actually your good work, Boss," said Jones.

Avery smiled as he struggled to interpret the meaning behind Jones' comment. Any doubt as to a potential error on his part was quickly dispelled as Jones expanded upon his compliment.

"I was told by the officers who were with you at Bare's apartment how quickly you locked down the scene before that bloody cleaner cleared up all the evidence."

"I just wanted to make sure the integrity was preserved, anyway I don't think I did a great job, you probably found my elimination prints all over," apologised Avery. "So what the hell happened there to poor Julia?"

"Early days, but I think we have to now classify her death as suspicious and formally link the incidents," said Jones.

"So the McKenzies maybe went after Sebastian but found Julia home alone?" speculated Avery.

"It's one explanation, but we simply don't know," replied Jones accurately.

"Okay, there's one question I need you to answer, Gareth, please tell me that Bare has nothing to do with what went on at the lock-up?"

"Already ahead of you, sir, we are fast-tracking an enquiry at his hotel in London and doing cell site analysis on his phone, it may be that he is also going to be alibied by the analyst he was visiting."

"What, in the middle of the night?" said a surprised Avery and then, "Oh, of course," as an afterthought when he remembered Robin.

The discussion was interrupted by Jones' phone vibrating impatiently and after apologising he answered it whilst indicating it was from the Incident Room.

Avery allowed Jones some privacy by standing up and walking

over to his favourite window spot. His favourite toy as a child had been a set of hand-painted puppets from a Punch and Judy show that had been performed by his grandfather for many years on their local beach. The officious policeman in the set had a black moustache and the resemblance between him and DCI Jones was uncanny. It was gratifying that after all these years he was still a skilled puppeteer.

His nostalgia was interrupted by DCI Jones revealing the McKenzies had even activated a speed camera after leaving the Bares' apartment.

"Let's hope we get a good image," said Avery.

"Afraid not, it's just a rear-view of the index in the dark, but with the direction of travel and time stamp it helps us with the chronology of the night," replied Jones.

"Well it sounds like it's all coming together. Okay, you obviously need to do an arrest strategy in relation to Sean McKenzie but let's not act until we have answers from London about DS Bare," ordered Avery.

"Agreed, I will update my Policy file and we will keep everything tight in the Incident Room," Jones concluded.

After Jones had left Avery telephoned the ACC to bring him up to speed with all the forensic revelations. As he expected the Chief Officer was more than happy for him to retain overall supervision of the two linked incidents under the proviso he was kept 'fully briefed'. In Avery's experience the most senior officers rarely liked to 'own' a problematic investigation for fear of it blowing up in their faces and jeopardising their ascent up the greasy pole. Of course when all landmines had been stepped on he had no doubt the ACC would emerge from his bunker to bask in the glory of a job well done. Avery had no ill feeling about this strategy and would have hated to have relinquished control of the delicious soap opera that was playing out before him. He had waited patiently before advancing to the next stage, but the delicious anticipation of some psychological torture was just too powerful to resist. He picked up his phone and visualised the dread the call recipient would soon be feeling.

CHAPTER 35

Morton had tidied the house before leaving. He emptied the contents of the stainless steel bin from the kitchen into the large, council-provided, blue wheelie bin standing to one side of the garage. He reflected that Stephanie hated performing this task although he realised that she would have to get used to it. The light rain turned into a downpour as he got into his car that purred into life as the ignition key was turned. He knew exactly where he was going and a brief check of the illuminated digital clock display confirmed he would arrive in plenty of time. The journey was made more problematic by the unrelenting rain that ran down the windscreen just as his tears flowed unabated down his cheeks. Morton began to take deep controlled breaths, trying to regain some level of composure. As he approached the slip road that led to the police station, his foot instinctively came off the accelerator in preparation for a left turn. The thought of driving the familiar route fleetingly entered his mind before he reapplied the accelerator and continued towards the ring road, gradually leaving the town lights in the rear-view mirror.

Twenty minutes later he arrived and parked the car in the deserted, small car park adjacent to the rail station. The clock display indicated 6.04pm meaning he had a thirteen-minute wait. Morton placed the sealed envelope that had been in his jacket pocket on the passenger seat before leaving the car. The central locking system made a loud clunking noise amplified by the night air as Morton walked away from the car. It had stopped raining which made it easier for Morton to light a cigarette as he walked towards the tiny unstaffed station. The only barrier to the platform was a small unlocked gate that creaked a small protest at Morton's push. He was surprisingly calm as he sat on the edge of the platform finishing the cigarette before easing himself down onto the tracks. He walked for about thirty yards until the illumination of the platform lights were left behind. As the darkness engulfed him, Detective Inspector Morton sat down in the middle of the train tracks and waited for the 6.17 train. Avery's call had left him in no doubt that he had been responsible for Julia Bare's death. He was at least grateful that he had been provided with the option to surrender himself to the Detective Superintendent rather than face the ignominy of being arrested at his home address. He had even briefly considered that option, but knew in his heart of hearts he was not brave enough to face the consequences. Although consumed by self-pity his last thoughts were those of regret for any anguish the train driver would later feel.

CHAPTER 36

The persistence of his ringing phone eventually woke Bare and his automatic glance at the bedside clock confirmed he had emerged from his first deep sleep in a week. He saw that it was Avery calling and the early hour made a significant update likely. After taking a deep breath he answered the phone with a perfunctory affirmation so as not to delay receipt of the news. Frustratingly, however, Avery was clearly unwilling to convey any information other than to summons him to his office.

The relatively short car journey preceded the rush hour so Bare arrived at the police station less than thirty minutes later. He saw Perkins standing by the rear door and as he approached him realised the junior officer had been posted there to await his arrival.

"What's going on?" Bare asked as he struggled to keep pace with his escort.

"No idea, Sarge, was just told to make sure you went straight to the top floor," came the honest reply.

Bare wondered whether others had been briefed ahead of him as a normally chatty uniform Inspector could only manage a murmured acknowledgement to Bare's greeting as they passed in the corridor. Any consideration that this was paranoia on his part was dispelled as even Ann looked hurriedly away as they passed through the secretary's office.

Once he had safely delivered his package to Avery, DC Perkins was immediately dismissed. Bare saw that his arrival had actually been awaited by three men who were now all looking at each other as if unsure as to who was to take the lead. Avery was the first to speak as he motioned for Bare to sit down.

"Thank you for coming in so quickly, Sebastian, you obviously know ACC Kent and DCI Jones."

"Blimey, it must be serious," replied Bare in an attempt to break the oppressive atmosphere apparent.

His mind was now in overdrive; clearly he was about to be the recipient of bad news but more worryingly, it was obviously going to be personal to him. He braced himself in anticipation of being told he was under arrest, knowing this to be illogical but it was the worst scenario he could imagine. For once his instincts were hopelessly wrong.

"Jim Morton died earlier this evening, Seb. I'm really sorry, I know you two went way back together. It appears at this stage that he took his own life."

Bare listened to the words but was unable to comprehend their meaning without repeating them back aloud.

"Jim's dead and he killed himself?"

He looked to Avery to deliver some more plausible meaning but only got a sombre nod by way of confirmation.

"That's bollocks. What happened? Jim would never do that. Why would he?" said Bare, shaking his head with disbelief but at the same time recognising Avery appeared to be fully confident in what he was saying.

Avery imparted the story without breaking his steady monotone delivery that he felt worked to best effect when delivering agony messages. He told Bare of the train driver's emergency call, the uniform response, the grim discovery of Morton's mutilated body, confirmation of his identity and the fact his vehicle was nearby.

Bare found himself challenging every aspect of the account he was hearing but Avery was able to present a compelling factual account of Morton's last movements.

"Jim would never kill himself," Bare reasserted. Whilst he was beginning to accept his friend's death, the events leading up to it appeared much less clear to him.

"There was a note in his car," said Avery, immediately extinguishing Bare's surfacing belief that someone else must have pushed his friend in front of the oncoming train.

"Does Stephanie know?" asked Bare.

"Yes, I am afraid I was saddled with that job," interjected Kent who immediately reddened in response to his own clumsy comment.

Whilst still struggling to process the news Bare began at least to understand West's presence in the meeting. He could not fathom why Jones was also there though and stared at him quizzically.

Jones in turn looked to Avery and received a consenting nod.

"Seb, I am here because there have also been some significant developments concerning Julia."

"Are going to tell me she definitely killed herself too?" challenged Bare.

"No I'm not, we are now treating her death as suspicious because we know she was not alone that night," replied Jones.

Bare closed his eyes and exhaled a deep breath upon hearing the first sentence in the meeting he believed to be true. The room fell silent again as the others waited for him to regain his composure. Recognising that his body language was delaying the receipt of information he was desperate to hear Bare sat forward and took another deep breath.

"Tell me everything," he said in the calmest voice he could muster.

It took an hour to fully brief him and he felt like a boxer trapped in the corner of the ring as one heavyweight blow followed another. Avery had anticipated a reaction of anger as Bare learned of the McKenzie connection but the shock of learning about the connected deaths seemed to anaesthetise the bereaved husband. Determined to provoke some reaction Avery concluded with a hypothesis about the reasons behind Morton's suicide.

"I think it's only fair you should know, Seb, that prior to Jim's death I received anonymous information that he was working with the McKenzies and had been supplying them with information, including your home address. He was due to come in and be interviewed regarding the allegations when he—"

Avery smiled inwardly as Bare didn't allow him to complete the sentence.

"Absolute bollocks," he had shouted before storming out of the office, unable to process any further revelations.

After a moment relishing the oppressive silence now engulfing his office Avery swivelled his chair in the direction of his stunned colleagues.

"Totally understandable, that poor, poor man. We need to get a liaison officer alongside him straightaway."

"It's already in hand, DS Sharon Brady is en route, I think she may know Seb from way back," reassured Jones.

CHAPTER 37

She found him on the roof of the station. The flat terraced area that had been transformed into a garden retreat had been the brainwave of a previous Chief Constable to provide staff with a tranquil alternative to the stresses and strains of policework. Ironically, the project had caused the Chief Officer more stress than any other aspect of his work as taxpayers learned of the project and used the tabloid press to question the Constabulary's priorities. Less officers on the beat but third place in the national Towns in Bloom contest was hardly a trade off the local Policy Authority could comfortably defend. The Chief Officer elected to enjoy the obscurity of retirement rather than endure continued public ridicule and the once highly maintained rooftop garden evolved into a smokers' retreat populated by the odd plant in the remaining ornamental urns.

Bare was leaning against the ornate barrier that deterred suicidal cops from jumping to their certain death and the serious likelihood of damaging a parked patrol car. He was smoking his third cigarette in succession and taking in the view of the busy town that stretched out to the horizon before him. He didn't acknowledge Sharon Brady as she joined him at the barrier. Despite learning of her appointment earlier, Bare had not decided how to receive his former lover. It had been eight years since he had seen her last and they had not parted on the best of terms. In fact, he found himself subliminally touching his jaw as she approached, the echo of his slapped face evoking a memory.

The two stood in silence, for what seemed like an eternity to them both, before DS Brady's sense of duty compelled her to speak.

"How are you doing, Bare?"

Bare found himself grateful for the soft tone in her voice and he sensed there was some genuine feeling to her question.

"I've had better weeks," he replied whilst turning to face her.

Her hair was styled differently but she had retained the same sharp dress sense that reflected a bright, enquiring mind. He remembered her philosophy about 'power dressing' as an effective weapon against the male-dominated culture of policing. She was of course correct in her assertion that it was more difficult for a woman to progress in the service, although Bare never acknowledged that to her during their brief relationship.

"So you have been sent in by Avery to apply the gentle touch?" asked Bare.

"No, of course not," snapped Brady.

"Shame, cause I seem to remember that you had a very nice gentle touch," said Bare, reinforcing the words with a soft stroke of Brady's arm.

Brady immediately pulled away.

"For fuck's sake, your wife's just been murdered, you bastard."

Bare smiled and Brady realised he had won the first point of their mind game. She had forgotten what an opponent he was when it came to mental combat.

"Ah, will the real Ms. Brady please stand up?" said the satisfied Bare.

"Okay, okay," said Brady, holding up her palms in a placatory gesture that contrasted her angry eyes.

"Can we start again?" she asked.

"Sure," said Bare. "So how have you been?"

To her surprise, Brady felt her anger ebb away as she provided Bare with a brief résumé of her life "post-affair" as she phrased it. She had kept in occasional contact with her friends while she was in Bermuda. They fell into two camps. Those who knew of her relationship with Bare made no mention of him and she never asked. But those who were oblivious of her real reason for seeking the secondment were subjected to veiled enquiries as to his welfare. It annoyed her that she retained a desire for information and couldn't fully understand her need to pick at a still painful scab.

Bare listened, genuinely saddened at the obvious adverse effect their relationship had caused. It had started with his pursuit of forbidden fruit, an older woman, a rank above him and married to a local solicitor. As a young single man he had mistaken her growing affection for him as being founded in lust rather than love. He had therefore been totally unprepared when she had left the stability of her marriage and arrived on his doorstep with two suitcases and an expectation of a new life together with her lover. She of course had immediately realised her mistake upon seeing his reaction and although he never vocalised it they both knew that signalled the end of their relationship. When she later told him of her successful secondment opportunity he of course had tried to disguise his palpable relief with a token request for her to stay but they both knew it was a final act of theatre in their short performance together.

"I had heard you were back and was going to give you a call to catch up," offered Bare.

"Yeah well it's only been six months. I expect you have been busy," replied Brady, putting down a marker about the blind acceptance of empty platitudes.

"So did you volunteer to babysit me?" he enquired.

"Let's just say I thought you would be needing some tough love. I am really sorry about Julia," she replied and the sincerity of her tone made Bare regret his churlish comment.

"Can you persuade Avery to let me work the case? I mean I know he won't let me near the sharp end but I need to do something."

"He has already said he wants you on compassionate leave, Seb, but I think we can make a case for you to be doing something if that's what you really want?"

"I will go stir crazy if I am not doing something, but just not some crap admin duty, OK?"

Satisfied that Bare was at least prepared to compromise she promised to speak to Avery on his behalf. Feeling the chill of the wind on the roof she offered him a canteen coffee in order to return to the indoor warmth of the police station and he dutifully followed as she made her way towards the door that provided access to the stairwell. Any complacency regarding the ease of her liaison role quickly evaporated when she heard his comment that after the drink he intended to visit Stephanie Morton.

CHAPTER 38

As a bemused Sean McKenzie was led away from the house in handcuffs he doubted that his impending interrogation by the police could be as ferocious as the one delivered by his mother in the wake of his brother's death. Mary McKenzie was desperately trying to understand the sequence of events that had led to the fatal fire and the subsequent orphan status of her grandson when she had seen the marked police cars arrive. Initially she had hoped they were bringing news of her son and daughter-in-law's murder but the officers' aggressive demeanour and demand for Sean's surrender had left her bewildered. She had listened in disbelief as her sole surviving son had been arrested on suspicion of Julia Bare's murder and had sought some understanding from the officers as they had led him away. The look on Sean's face had been enough to tell a mother that he was genuinely shocked and any fleeting fear that he was indeed a murderer quickly left her. Instead she had held her grandson with the tightest hug she could summons and tried to ignore the remaining officers searching every square inch of her property.

She had held the front door open to facilitate the exit of the last officers as they carried away the majority of her son's clothes in evidence bags and had reflected how quickly the McKenzies had lost their brief 'victim' status before being recast in the more familiar criminal role. Only when she had been sure the last police car had disappeared from sight had she allowed the tears to run unabated down her cheeks and she wept for the first time since Stuart's death.

The sound of her ringing phone made her regain some composure and she took the incoming call from her nephew. Patrick McKenzie delivered his news with a calm professionalism that she had grown accustomed to over the years. Had he not referred to her as Aunt Mary at the start of the conversation any third party listening in would have presumed it was a normal call to a client from their accountant. It quickly became apparent that the arrest of Sean had been carefully synchronised with other police 'visits' to properties associated with the McKenzie dynasty and the subsequent seizure of financial records. Despite Patrick's reassurances that he was confident nothing incriminating had been taken the scale of the operation left Mary in no doubt that the family were in the eye of a storm. After thanking him for the update and passing on the news of his cousin's incarceration Mary retrieved her other phone from its hasty temporary hiding place in her underwear. She quickly rang Morton's number and screamed in frustration as once again it immediately diverted to his monotone voicemail.

She made two further calls, one to the family solicitor to ensure Sean's immediate representation and the other to a family friend requesting they come babysit Cameron as she had an urgent errand to run. As soon as the friend arrived Mary got into her car and the screech of the wheels on the gravel drive left no one in doubt that she was on a mission.

The forty-minute drive did provide her with valuable time to regain some calm perspective and she decided to stop short of the address and formulate a better plan than knocking on the Detective Inspector's front door. The local radio station that had been mere background noise during her journey suddenly made her reach for the volume button. She listened with astonishment as the intended recipient of her visit was confirmed as the identity of a man killed by a train. Mary closed her eyes and drew a deep breath as she tried to assess the implications of the suicide for her and the family.

After a few minutes of contemplation she reached for the burner phone nestled in a side pocket of her cluttered bag. She tapped the number quickly but hesitated on the last digit; the rapidly unfolding events had made her doubt her own judgement. Finally she pressed the number and heard the briefest of ring tones before the call was answered by the police station switchboard operator.

"Could you put me through to Detective Sergeant Bare please?" she enquired.

There was no affirmation from the operator but she heard another ringtone that indicated her call had indeed been transferred. She drew a deep breath, still uncertain as to her first sentence but the recorded voicemail greeting of Sebastian Bare prevented any continuance of her thought and she quickly terminated the call. Whatever her communication would have entailed was uncertain but she was sure it was inappropriate to leave a recorded message. With her heart still beating faster due to the adrenaline rush of making that call she instead turned the car engine back on and headed for home. She felt a long hug with her grandson would be mutually beneficial.

CHAPTER 39

"Are you sure about this?" asked Brady as they walked up the pathway towards the front door.

"I need to pay my respects," said Bare, unsure whether he was justifying the visit to Brady or himself.

There was no response to Bare's loud knock on the door but much to Brady's disappointment her colleague was undeterred. His height allowed him to reach over the side gate and unbolt it which facilitated their access to the impeccably maintained garden. If Stephanie Morton saw them approach the conservatory she didn't acknowledge their presence, remaining seated on the wicker sofa, lost in her thoughts. Bare hesitated for a moment as he observed her almost catatonic state, immediately recognising it as a side effect of grief. He looked to Brady for some guidance as to whether to proceed but then elected to ignore her gesticulation to leave. His tap on the conservatory window startled Stephanie and she sprang to her feet with surprising speed. It took her a moment to recognise one of the people staring at her from the sanctuary of her rear garden and she opened the door to allow Bare and the woman inside.

Brady stood awkwardly unintroduced as Stephanie and Bare immediately embraced without speaking. When they parted Brady could see both had tears in their eyes and she was at least relieved that the greeting had diluted any anger that may have motivated Bare to visit. Stephanie motioned for the pair to sit down and Bare took the opportunity to introduce the women to each other. When his description of Brady as a Family Liaison Officer had received a confused look from Stephanie, he rephrased the title as 'babysitter to keep him out of trouble' and the three shared a smile. After apologising for not immediately offering them a cup of tea Stephanie acquiesced to Brady's offer to go put the kettle on. When she returned minutes later with three full mugs on a tray she was unsurprised to find the pair in deep conversation, each seeking answers to seemingly impossible questions.

Bare listened intently as Stephanie recounted how she had learned of her husband's death and then her shock at being told he was under investigation for alleged corruption. Bare feigned surprise that Stephanie had received a visit from officers from the Professional Standards Department who had conducted a search of the house and had casually asked whether they had found anything despite Brady's very obvious glare of disapproval.

"I just don't understand it, Seb, you know Jim was as straight and ethical as anyone could be and to suggest he had any involvement in Julia…" She didn't complete the sentence but it was obvious to Bare that Professional Standards had been remarkably frank in their disclosures.

"I know Jim would have never knowingly caused any harm to Julia," he said, taking hold of Stephanie's hand for additional emphasis.

"But it's such a mess," said a now sobbing Stephanie. "You are the only friend or colleague to have had the decency to come around, it's like Jim is being portrayed as a monster."

"Hey, nobody who knew Jim thinks that for one minute,"

reassured Bare. "The whole nick is just as confused as you are."

"And he was so upset for you about Julia, we both were," she said, now holding onto his hand as firmly as he had held hers.

"Thank you, that means a lot. I promise you I will get all the answers, Steph," said Bare, deliberately ignoring Brady's non-verbal rebuke that had been made out of Stephanie's sight.

"You know he left a note," she continued without acknowledging Bare's promise.

"Yes I heard that, but obviously the bosses didn't divulge the contents to me," replied Bare, grateful that Stephanie had raised the subject without any prompt.

"They wouldn't let me keep it because they were checking it for fingerprints I think, but I read it and it was definitely Jim's handwriting," she continued.

"I hope it told you something," he said, almost feeling the disapproval radiating from Brady.

"I wrote it down," she said whilst retrieving the much-read crumpled piece of paper from her pocket and handed it to Bare.

'Dearest Steph, I am truly sorry. I hope the stigma of being married to me won't destroy your life too. You don't deserve that. I have left my wedding ring at home for you because I didn't want anyone else to have it, even for a moment. Be strong, love always, Jim.'

Bare struggled to hide his disappointment; whatever content he had been hoping for in the note wasn't there. He handed the note to Brady to confirm that he had not gained any insight into the investigation he was precluded from.

"I should have known something was wrong when I got home and saw his wedding ring on the table, he had even put it on a keyring so I didn't miss it."

"I guess he just wanted to make sure you got it," said Bare.

"Yes and it reminds me, I need to cancel his golf club membership," she added.

"Err, okay," he replied, unable to fathom the connection.

"Sorry, I am not making any sense," Stephanie continued. "The keyring he used had a key on it, to his locker at the golf club."

"Oh I see," said Bare, "and did you mention that to the Professional Standards officers?" he added as casually as he could. She shook her head in response before retreating to the kitchen to make another drink whilst having another private weep. When she returned Bare apologised that the officers would not have time to drink it as they had been called away. He suspected she knew this to be false but even in the midst of her grief knew she would be far too polite to challenge his excuse to leave. Instead she hugged and thanked him for the visit before offering more condolences about Julia.

They sat in silence for the first mile of the journey away from Stephanie's house before Brady's frustration got the better of her.

"That was nothing but a fishing trip, what part of 'not to be involved in the investigation' don't you understand?"

"You heard her, no one from the job has had the decency to go near her, I was just offering support to someone in a similar position to me."

"So you going to hand it in then?" she asked pointedly.

"Hand what in?"

"The locker key that you obviously got off her when you went back for your phone that you 'accidentally' left on her sofa," she replied, recalling her impatient wait in the car a few minutes earlier.

Bare knew it was futile to protest his innocence as he remembered how intuitive Brady had been during their relationship.

"She asked me to clear his bloody locker out because she didn't want to face it, what's the problem with that?"

"Are you going to hand it in?" she repeated.

"Look, we virtually have to drive past the place, let's pop in and collect his tartan plus fours and if there is anything remotely suspicious there, which there won't be, we can take it back to the nick as an example of the Unprofessional Standards Department."

"You are an arsehole," she said flatly, looking out of the car window at the scenic countryside.

CHAPTER 40

Despite his reassurance that it would be a fleeting visit she declined his offer to wait in the car in order not to be soaked by the sudden downpour. The golf club car park was sufficiently far from the clubhouse to ensure they both got wet despite their undignified heroic sprint that was exacerbated by the incorrect selection of the right entrance. Their bedraggled appearance and breathless introduction to the steward caused him to peruse the warrant cards for a longer time than he ordinarily would have before he permitted entry to the members only section of the club. As they reached the changing rooms Bare pointed out the austere 'Men only' sign above the door and Brady wondered if her very presence in the building was causing multiple grave revolutions of original members.

"Unless you want to see a lot of naked geriatric men you had best wait here," said Bare as he pushed open the heavy oak door. Initially she was going to protest but a quick glance over his shoulder confirmed his warning as she saw an elderly man drying his hair with the towel that he had removed from his waist.

"Don't be long," she hissed whilst folding her arms and leaning back against the wall.

It took him a while to locate the locker as the ornate numbers on the front were not sequential but he eventually found it close to the shower entrance. As he inserted the key and heard the satisfying release click of the lock, it occurred to him to him that he and Morton had never talked about golf. He had assumed that membership of this exclusive club was merely another status symbol that dear old Jim seemed drawn to but it suddenly occurred to him that he might have actually enjoyed the sport. The unanswered question nagged him as he opened the locker door and provided another example of not knowing his former friend as well as he had always presumed.

The locker was of a traditional design with the interior divided into two sections, a small compartment at the top and a larger one below with a clothes rail. There were a number of toiletries neatly arranged in the top including a bottle of aftershave that Bare immediately recognised as the brand Morton always wore. A quick spray into the air released the evocative scent that he associated with his friend and caused him to pause, still coming to terms with the fact that Morton appeared to have been inextricably linked with Julia's death. The entrance of a golfer into the changing room reminded him that an impatient Brady was waiting on the other side of the door and he resumed his search. A set of waterproofs were the only clothes hanging inside and the only other item apparent was a brown leather sports holdall covering the base of the locker. Bare removed it and could see that it only appeared to contain a pair of spiked golf shoes. Closer examination of the bag revealed it to be a purpose-constructed golf accessory with a separate zip-fastened bottom section specifically for shoes so as to keep the remainder of the bag mud free. The weight of the bag suggested something else was inside this compartment and Bare rested it on a wooden bench as he unzipped that section. A quick glimpse of the contents caused him to immediately zip the bag back up and a glance around reassured him that the discovery had not been witnessed by the other men in his proximity. Bare then emptied the remaining items of the locker into the bag's main section and after removing the door key walked casually toward the exit.

Brady's expectant look was met by him holding up the holdall and showing her the contents of the main section.

"Waterproofs, shoes and a bottle of Old Spice," was his summary of the contents held out for her inspection which she declined.

"It was worth a look," he said philosophically as he threw the bag with distain onto the back seat of the car. "I don't suppose you would drop it round to Steph's sometime for me?"

"Nope, you offered to go collect it," she replied.

"Okay, fair enough," he replied, looking away at the same time in case she saw any relief in his otherwise impassive expression.

CHAPTER 41

The adrenalin rush of the previous week's events had now subsided and Avery was left feeling tired and irritable. He tried to alter his mindset by reflecting how delicious it had been to execute his plan. A wonderful combination of pre-planned events supplemented by the thrill of the unpredictable improvisation he had employed. He had delighted when his inferior subordinates had attempted to make sense of the chaos he had caused and had skilfully nudged them along until they had arrived at the 'truth'.

ACC Kent had insisted that he accompany him to the briefing of the Chief Constable and Police and Crime Commissioner but he was under no illusion as to his expected role. Kent was clearly going to take the credit for the whole investigation and he was expected to play the supporting role and be on hand in case the ACC forgot salient facts. Avery wondered whether the briefing recipients were more astute than the ACC but he doubted it. His limited interaction with them suggested they were all cut from the same cloth and would lap up Kent's monologue so they in turn could plagiarise it later for their own gain.

The sudden silence in the room and the quizzical looks in his direction confirmed Avery had become too enveloped in his own thoughts and had missed a question aimed in his direction.

"Are we keeping you up, Mr Avery?" asked the Chief.

"Am so sorry, sir, as you can imagine it's been a tiring few days and despite Mr Kent's support I haven't managed to see my bed for a couple of days," replied the Superintendent.

"Yes of course, that wasn't very gracious of me," said a reddening Chief and then with admirable dexterity diverted the blame toward his Assistant. "Why have you dragged Paul here?"

"Err, well I thought it was important in case you had any specific questions, sir," stuttered Kent, annoyed that the concession of Avery's importance undermined his own position.

"Well are we any closer to finding out who killed the McKenzie couple or not?" asked the Chief.

"No, I am afraid not, obviously we are working through all the enquiries but nothing definitive as yet," replied Kent in apologetic tones.

"Actually we have a breakthrough today," interjected Avery, focusing on the Chief and ignoring Kent's puzzled look in his peripheral vision. "I chased up Forensic Science Services and they have established a ballistics link to the gun used to shoot Liam McKenzie. The same gun was used in a shooting in London a few years ago when an Albanian drug supplier was executed. The murder is unsolved but thought to be down to a rival drug group."

"So what's your hypothesis, Paul?" asked the Chief, realising now which of his subordinates was actually running the investigation.

"Well we know the McKenzies were expanding their drug business. I think it's likely they upset one of the bigger groups and this was payback, I think it's just a coincidence it happened shortly after they killed Julia Bare," surmised Avery and then as an afterthought he turned back toward Kent. "Sorry sir, I didn't have a chance to brief you prior to this meeting."

Kent held up his palms in a placatory gesture in the knowledge that his attempt to take credit for the investigation had crashed fatally on the rocks.

The Chief leaned back in his leather swivel chair apparently contemplating the freshly received update. After a few seconds to process the information he turned to the Commissioner and asked for his thoughts.

"I think we can spin this to our advantage," said the Commissioner, whose reason for being in the briefing became abundantly clear. "Public confidence is clearly the most important objective here, we just need to emphasise how quickly we have dealt with this and keep the focus on maintaining support. Perhaps arrange a memorial for Julie Bare, keep the sympathy story going."

"It's Julia Bare," interjected Avery, unable to resist the opportunity to interrupt the blatant electioneering the Commissioner was proposing.

"Yes, quite so," agreed the Commissioner, apparently impervious to the name correction, "and let's make sure that we use DI Morton as our scapegoat, good result all round I would say."

Avery nodded in agreement, immune to the callous politics of policing and wondered whether he had singlehandedly assured the re-selection of the Crime Commissioner at the forthcoming local elections. The grey-haired self-serving politician might prove to be a useful ally in Avery's career progression, he decided, so made a mental note to engineer a future meeting to cement a relationship.

CHAPTER 42

Sean McKenzie had never wanted to speak so much during a police interview but the intense stare from his solicitor ensured he only repeated the same two words.

"No comment," he said again.

Unperturbed, the interviewing officers carried on asking him questions about his involvement in the death of a woman he was fairly confident he had never met. When they presented evidence suggesting he had been at the crime scene he looked to his solicitor for guidance as he knew he had never been in the building they were describing. His solicitor's understated silent shake of the head made him reluctantly vocalise the by now monotonous response.

When the interview concluded he was left alone with his solicitor in the same room for a private consultation.

"I am being stitched up, why didn't you let me speak?"

"We have been through that, Sean, it's not up to us to disprove the case, it's up to them to prove it," replied John Watkins who had represented most of the McKenzie family over his twenty-eight-year career in the legal profession.

"But I never did anything this time," asserted McKenzie.

"Well then there is no reason to be concerned," reassured

Watkins. "As far as I can see the main bulk of their evidence is against your brother, the only thing they have on you is the sighting of your vehicle nearby and some trace evidence on a cigarette butt."

"But I never went there and if I had I wouldn't have left a bloody cigarette stub," said McKenzie, apparently aggrieved at the assertion of his guilt and professional competence as a criminal.

"Quite, which is why we need to remain calm and considered, now I need the names of those persons who will provide you with an alibi as to your movements that night," said Watkins when his expensive pen poised over a virgin page in his notebook.

"Me brother and Shannon dropped me off in town about just after five, they were driving my car, how can I remember who I saw that night? I was bladdered by eight o'clock."

"Look, Sean, it's important we show where you were and who you were with, think hard and give me some names," countered Watkins, already dreading the update he would be required to provide to the formidable Mrs McKenzie.

"I went to the Kings and met up with Marvellous and Georgie boy. Probably Tommy and his cousin was there though it might have been later we saw them at the Selkirk with Gastro and Welchy, then some of us went to Ritzys," recounted McKenzie at speed which only served to exaggerate his Scottish accent.

Watkins raised his hand to stop the flow of indecipherable words.

"You went to the Kings Head Public House around 5pm and met someone called Marvellous and Georgie boy?" he checked.

"Aye, write that down," instructed McKenzie, not understanding why Watkins had yet to start taking notes.

"Who is Marvellous?" enquired his solicitor.

"That's not his real name," said McKenzie with unnecessary explanation and then after understanding the meaning of the prompt added, "His real name is Marvin but I don't know his last name 'cause everyone just calls him Marvellous."

"Okay," said Watkins as the enormity of his task began to sink in, "and do you know Georgie boy's surname?"

McKenzie's furrowed brow demonstrated he was trying to remember before he exclaimed, "Yes, it's Brown."

Watkins transcribed the name George Brown into his notebook only to cross it out moments later when McKenzie added, "But his real name isn't George, it's Gregory but he doesn't like that."

After an exhausting hour Watkins closed his notebook with a degree of confidence that he had recorded Sean McKenzie's alibi for the night of Julia Bare's murder.

"Obviously we will have to get statements from everyone you have named and I am sure we can secure some CCTV as well," concluded Watkins.

"Aye and if you need any more am sure a few of my other mates would help out, though I doubt you will find any CCTV 'cause the places I go tend not to have it for security reasons," added McKenzie without the slightest degree of irony in his voice. "And before you ask I didn't have my phone turned on all night because it can be tracked, you know."

"By the Police, yes I know," said Watkins.

"No, by my ma, she made me put an app on the thing," said an indignant McKenzie.

CHAPTER 43

Bare walked straight into the lounge and hurriedly tipped the contents of the holdall onto the floor. Content nothing was left in the main section he quickly unzipped the lower compartment and removed all of the bulky envelopes. They were all sealed except the one he had first seen in the changing room with the tight wad of banknotes clearly visible. He started with that one and carefully removed the notes that appeared to be mostly of £20 denomination. He wet his right thumb with his tongue and proceeded to count the money. Only when he had finished did he audibly exhale while leaning back on the comfortable sofa. The envelope contained two thousand pounds and a quick scan of the other unopened ones indicated they were all of the same size and thickness. There were twenty-eight envelopes in total suggesting Morton had been concealing fifty-six thousand pounds in his golf club locker.

It was only when Bare opened the second envelope to confirm his estimate of the total inside did he notice the annotation in black ink on the inside of the top flap. Although there were only a few numbers and initials written down he immediately recognised the writing as being that of Morton having seen numerous statements and reports written by the same hand. Bare carefully inspected each of the envelopes in turn and noted a similar inscription on each one.

The code wasn't exactly difficult to decipher as it appeared to show a date, an amount (2k) and a set of initials which were always the same namely 'SM'. Bare placed the envelopes in a line to show their chronological order and it was only at that point that he saw the envelope that was the most recently dated had slightly different initials. He held it under a light to double check but was sure that envelope spelt 'MM' rather than 'SM'. Bare then returned to the notes in the first few envelopes and realised the contents slightly differed in that the images adorning the rear of the older notes were of Shakespeare and Faraday rather than the modern depictions of lesser known economists.

It appeared that whilst James Morton had been in the employ of the McKenzie family for numerous years he had never spent any of his ill-gotten gains and Bare felt a wave of empathy for his former friend. After pouring himself a large drink Bare stood over the haul in quiet contemplation before repacking the holdall with its less incriminating contents. He put the money in a separate plastic bag and carried both down to his car. Within thirty minutes he was again knocking on Stephanie Morton's door but on this occasion she deemed to answer it. He declined her offer to go inside but instead apologetically handed her the holdall that had belonged to her late husband.

"What's in it?" she asked.

"It's just some clothes, golf shoes and toiletries," he answered truthfully.

"Well thank you, Seb, that was really kind and it has saved me a job."

After receiving a hug of gratitude he drove away from the house with the full plastic bag in the passenger footwell. The bag he had chosen at random from his kitchen had a cartoon character of a dog on it that now seemed to be giving him a reproachful stare so when he came to a temporary stop at some red traffic lights he turned the bag around.

CHAPTER 44

Avery walked into the small office without knocking, causing Bare and Brady to instantly stop talking. Unapologetic for the interruption Avery dispensed with the formalities of a greeting and asked Bare how his work was progressing. Bare understood that any criticism of his assigned task would not be well received by the Superintendent so restricted his reply to, "Okay thanks."

Realising the brevity of the reply would not appease the senior officer's enquiry Brady quickly stepped in with more detail.

"As you know, sir, we are doing a cold case review on the Vickers murder so at the moment it's just a matter of trying to get up to speed with all the paperwork. Sadly it's not exactly in good order."

She pointed to an array of box files and a large box that appeared to contain loose photographs and other sundry items collected by the original enquiry team. Avery picked up a photograph that depicted the burnt out remains of Vickers' car and remembered the satisfying way it had ignited.

"I remember this case, was just before I left for the Met, remind me who the SIO was?"

"It was a DCI Godfrey, unfortunately he died a few years after retiring," replied Brady, anticipating Avery's supplemental question as to whether he had been debriefed.

"I remember Jack Godfrey, very old school, what was his nickname again?"

"Friday," answered Bare.

"Why Friday?" asked Brady with genuine curiosity.

"Because if Jack said it was Friday it was bloody Friday," replied the men in unison and smiled at the memory of the bombastic detective.

"Simpler times, no computers, very basic forensic support, it's a wonder anything got detected," reminisced Avery.

"Well this one didn't get solved," reminded Bare, "despite Gregory beating six bells out of a few suspects."

"Well let's hope we have better luck this time around, it's important work," said Avery in that condescending tone Bare associated with the majority of senior officers. After a generic enquiry as to the Sergeant's welfare Avery left apparently satisfied with his cursory inspection.

"It's important work," mimicked Bare when confident that Avery was no longer in audible range.

"It's better than sitting on your hands at home or doing some desk job, remember?" said Brady, irritated that Bare had not acknowledged her efforts in securing the position.

"Yes, guess so," came the grudging reply as Bare looked at the same photograph Avery had casually left to one side after viewing, "but it is a mess. I remember Gregory briefing the team that he would have it all sorted in a week."

"Did he have a theory?" asked Brady, grateful that at least Bare was now thinking about their assigned case.

"Vickers was an obnoxious small-time player, he just thought he had upset someone and if he rattled the tree hard enough the culprit would fall down at his feet. 'Slow' and 'methodical' weren't exactly words associated with Friday Godfrey!"

"So nobody specific in the frame?"

"No, we all held our own informants up against the wall but there was not even a whisper, pretty soon the Guvnors shut it down to save overtime costs, there wasn't exactly a public outcry over the demise of Simon Vickers."

"Well perhaps the answer is in that lot," said Brady, casting another rueful glance toward the box of papers that would necessitate extensive time to review and categorise.

"Yep, so if you want to make a start I will go and get the coffee in," said Bare, reaching for his jacket that he had draped over an empty office chair.

"Oh I think the initial sorting needs to be done by someone with a background knowledge of the case," said Brady, already striding toward the door. "White latte, no sugar?"

Bare knew from experience that this was a battle he could not win so merely requested the addition of a bacon roll as he tipped the contents of the box onto a large empty desk. The unceremonious manner of emptying the box caused some papers to fall onto the office floor and cursing his own clumsiness he stooped to pick the documents up. The first one he grasped was a typed information report from Detective Constable Morton and he smiled as he read the flowery language Jim had used in an effort to impress his supervisors. Bare sat back down in his chair looking at the signature adorning the report and felt a wave of loss. Whilst his own intuition had been tested over the preceding days he knew with some certainty that James Morton had not been a bad man and refused to accept he had knowingly contributed to Julia's death.

CHAPTER 45

Gareth Jones was not a man that easily lost his temper but the meeting with the Crown Prosecution Service had caused him to explode with rage following their decision there had been insufficient evidence to charge Sean McKenzie.

"We have got his bloody DNA at the scene," he repeated in a final futile attempt to change the mind of the reviewing lawyer.

"No, Detective Chief Inspector, you have his DNA on a single portable object found at the scene, a cigarette stub that could have been taken there accidentally by his brother on the bottom of his shoe. Besides, he has multiple witnesses providing him with an alibi."

"They are not credible witnesses, they are known associates," countered Jones, throwing his arms up in an exaggerated display of his disbelief at the decision.

"You need to find me some more evidence, at the moment there isn't a realistic prospect of conviction, I'm sorry," said the unmoved lawyer, symbolically closing his book to signal the end of their meeting.

Jones checked his watch as he left the building knowing that he had to communicate the decision urgently to the custody centre holding McKenzie. Despite the warrant of further detention being granted there was a limit as to how long a suspect could be held without being charged and this suspect was less than an hour away from that limit. He wondered how Sebastian Bare would take the news and decided that it was best for it to be delivered by Avery rather than himself. Thankfully the Detective Superintendent answered his phone immediately and appeared to be much more philosophical about the charging decision.

In reality Avery was considerably irked by the news as it meant an inevitable protraction of the investigation which he had promised to the Chief would be quickly resolved. Furthermore, it would allow the McKenzie family an opportunity to regroup when the actions he had instigated had taken their whole enterprise to the verge of collapse. Whilst he waited for the summonsed Bare to arrive in his office Avery considered his options. He thought about lighting the already short fuse of Bare in the hope that he would exact revenge on Sean McKenzie and briefly visualised his Sergeant in this role. Although tempted he was not convinced Bare had it in him to exact the type of revenge Avery was visualising and quickly dismissed the idea. Besides, there was also the risk of collateral damage to his own reputation as a perceived supervisor of renegade officers to consider. After a few minutes of cold, calculating analysis he decided that the better tactic was to merely inform Bare of the decision and give him the standard 'keep away from the investigation and suspect' warning. If nothing else that would at least distract him from his cold case review, not that Avery was particularly concerned the dynamic duo would discover anything the previous investigation had missed.

The knock at his door signalled Bare's arrival and the subsequent meeting between the two men went pretty much as Avery had anticipated. He had tried to show empathy at the right times as Bare went through the cycle of disbelief, indignation and anger. Whilst imparting his instruction to stay away from Sean McKenzie to an increasingly resentful Bare, Avery wondered what it really felt like to experience such a vast array of emotions. His conclusion was that aside from anything else it must be truly exhausting for the individual concerned judging by the amount of energy they apparently expended.

After he had walked Bare to the door and placed the obligatory hand of comfort on his shoulder, Avery returned to his desk and swivelled his chair toward the window. Another option occurred to him as he watched the scurrying creatures preoccupied with their insignificant lives at ground level below. He slowly circled a pen between his fingers, a subconscious action, as his idea gained traction.

Just as he was considering the finer detail his thoughts were interrupted by another knock at the door swiftly followed by the entrance of his Personal Assistant.

"What is it, Ann?" his tone barely concealing his irritation.

"You asked me to remind you that you have agreed to chair the Force Health and Safety Meeting this afternoon on behalf of the ACC," explained the ever efficient staff member.

"Oh damn, I completely forgot," said Avery, hurriedly grabbing a related ring binder from a nearby shelf. "Tell them I am en route," he muttered as he walked past her.

"Yes sir, of course," she replied. She didn't know exactly why but seeing her boss momentarily off guard caused her a certain amount of delight.

Avery didn't notice as he strode quickly down the corridor wondering how easy it would be to concentrate on chairing a mundane meeting when moments earlier he had been practically salivating at the prospect of murdering Sean McKenzie.

CHAPTER 46

Mary McKenzie was grateful to have her son home and wasted no time in conducting her own interview to determine his involvement in the murder of Sebastian Bare's wife. After an hour of discussion she was entirely satisfied that the only guilt he owned was his unknowing contribution to his brother's death. His explanation of the questions posed to him by the police interviewers left her shaking her head in disbelief around Liam's involvement in the same crime.

"It just makes no sense, how could he have done anything? He was with Shannon doing your stint at the lock-up," she said without meaning to emphasise Sean's causation of his brother's whereabouts.

"We both promised you, Ma, we wouldn't go after that copper, how would we even know where he lived?" Sean replied. "And if someone was setting us up why were Liam and Shannon killed?"

Mary remained silent as the unanswered question added to the many others swirling around her mind. The police were suggesting that it was a coincidence her late son was both a murderer and a victim within the space of a few hours in unrelated events, but her intuition was screaming this was untrue. The address where Julia Bare had died was indeed the one James Morton had passed to her but she had retained this information to herself and now he was dead too. For the first time she vocalised the only conclusion that made any sense to her.

"Some bastards are waging war on us and the police and are laughing at the chaos," she surmised.

Sean looked at his mother with the expectation she would expand on her theory but to his growing confusion she didn't. Instead he recognised the familiar fire in her eyes that signified she was about to embark on a mission.

"I don't want you leaving the house, whoever killed Liam is still out there. Do you understand?" she said in an authoritative tone.

He nodded in silent response. In truth his time in custody and the enormity of events had left him shattered and he was just craving the solitude of his bed.

"Good, I need to go out," she said, putting on her jacket.

"Do you want me to come with you, Ma? It may not be safe for you either," he said without really understanding why.

She tenderly touched his cheek and looked into his eyes.

"You should know by now that no one would ever dare come for Mary McKenzie," she reassured and he instantly knew that to be true.

She checked her watch and hoped she would beat the rush hour traffic as she walked briskly towards her car. There was a courteous exchange of nods as she passed the men sitting in the car outside her home, hired help to ensure there were no unwelcome visitors to disturb what remained of her family inside. Then she drove in the hope that by the time she reached her destination she would have formulated the right words for the conversation she never wished to have.

Her heart was racing by the time she had parked her car and walked into the small public house. She had never been in that particular premises before and was gratified that it was at least a modern bar with decent-looking clientele. Despite her confidence she had never liked walking alone into a licensed premises, irritated that the same action probably wouldn't cause a member of the opposite sex a moment's hesitation. Thankfully the early evening customers were sparse and after ordering her drink she sat alone at the table that provided her with the best vantage point of the apartment block opposite. She again checked her watch and wondered how long she might have to wait before he arrived home or whether indeed he was even still living there. The red wine she was slowly sipping was at least helping her heart slow to a regular rhythm and she wondered if Stuart would have handled the matter in the same way. She felt some belated guilt concerning the way she had acted at the end of his life and having reflected on it, now understood that his actions were motivated by love. As she swirled the last remaining wine around the bottom of the glass memories of happier times made her eyes begin to water and she brushed away the emerging tear. She was about to order another drink when she saw someone approach the apartment entrance. The artificial lighting around the area made the identification more difficult but after a few seconds she was sure enough to leave the pub and walk briskly across the road.

After entering the building she saw him waiting patiently for the summonsed lift to arrive at the ground floor. He had his back to her and was considerably taller so she had to reach up to tap him on the shoulder. The action caused him to instantly turn around and his confused expression caused her to introduce herself despite them having first met years before.

"Hello DS Bare, I'm Mary McKenzie and I really need to speak to you," she said with a calm authority that masked her rising trepidation.

CHAPTER 47

Having quickly recovered from the initial shock of meeting her on his own doorstep Bare's reaction was not the hostile one she had anticipated. He had baulked at first at the suggestion he should invite her inside but unable to suppress his curiosity as to the reason for the meeting, he had acquiesced, even performing the courtesy of holding the front door open to allow her access first. As she walked toward the lounge she took her jacket off and casually handed it to him and he dutifully hung it on a set of hooks inside the hallway.

"What do you want?" he said.

"That's very nice of you, Sebastian, I will have a scotch please and you had better pour yourself one," came the unexpected reply.

He shook his head but nevertheless took two glasses from a cupboard and poured a generous amount of whisky in both.

"Ice?" he asked.

"And dilute God's own nectar? I think not," she retorted as the glass was taken without thanks.

Bare took a sip from his own glass and took a moment to study the woman. He knew she was in her early sixties but her posture was that of a younger woman. She was probably a shade over five feet tall but the heels she was wearing together with the simple lines of her designer outfit made her appear considerably taller. But most of all he noticed those piercing green eyes that were now staring at him as she prepared to forgo further foreplay.

"I know you won't accept this but my boys had nothing to do with your wife's death," she announced.

"Well thanks for stopping by and clearing that up," he replied, using sarcasm to mask his growing temper.

"Somebody is trying to frame them and I think the same people killed my Liam," she continued and for the first time in the encounter Bare saw a flicker of emotion cross her face as she mentioned her dead son by name.

"Well that's certainly an interesting theory, but really you should be talking to the Major Investigation Team and not the husband of the innocent victim who was thrown off that fucking balcony," he snapped, pointing theatrically towards the place where Julia had been executed.

"I can't talk to anyone else and if you give me ten minutes of your time I will explain why, after that it's up to you."

Her new softer tone calmed Bare who despite his bravado was desperate to know what had motivated her unexpected visit. He gestured for her to sit down but to remove any doubt as to who was in control he made an obvious gesture to check his watch.

"Ten minutes," was his cold reply.

"Sebastian, my family is under attack and I am genuinely fearful for what might happen next. At the moment I don't trust anyone, especially the police but I am guessing you want to know who murdered your wife as much as I want to know who killed Liam and Shannon."

"Have you asked Sean?" asked Bare, uncaring as to how many

legal protocols he was probably breaking.

"I have known when that boy has been lying for the last thirty years and he wasn't involved, in fact he would be incapable of doing harm to a woman," she asserted.

"Yeah well the prisons are full of sons of doting mothers, nine minutes left."

"Liam had a dark side but it was you he would have liked to hurt, not your wife," she said.

"Oh, you don't seem as sure about son number one's innocence then," observed Bare.

"I am a hundred percent sure. The boys made a solemn vow not to come after you and had no idea where you lived."

"Ah, but that's wrong, isn't it, because you had your little spy in the camp, didn't you?" said Bare.

"Yes, we had James Morton talking to us for a long time and yes, he gave me this address but that remained with me and me alone."

Bare was an experienced interrogator and was surprised how quickly the woman had admitted her part in police corruption but he was anxious to press home the point.

"So why did you ask him where I lived?"

"Because he told me about Operation Spider, he told me he would derail it but I needed him to believe there would be a consequence if he didn't," she replied.

"How the fuck did you turn the straightest cop I have ever worked with?" asked Bare.

"It's a long story and I wish Stuart was here to provide you with the finer detail but I think essentially we exploited a vulnerability.

Isn't that how you recruit informants, Sebastian?"

Bare shook his head slowly and was visibly annoyed at the comparison.

"You see Stuart was a very astute man, Sebastian, and was merely putting in place a measure to stop the police from using the same tactic against us, like you already had done to catch my boys doing that stupid robbery."

"I have no idea what you are talking about," replied Bare.

"Stuart didn't believe in coincidences, you see, and the fact that two young ambitious detectives were in the exact spot when the boys were committing that robbery just never rang true for him, it was like a scab that he had to keep picking."

Bare remained silent after deciding to allow her to continue the story.

"It took him a while but he was a sly old fox and he got there in the end and after he confronted Shannon. She told him everything, she told him how the young detective had befriended her and promised her no one would ever know. Oh, and she told him how relieved she had been when Liam got locked up so she didn't have to suffer the beatings at his hand."

"Surely if Shannon had told him that she would have received some good old McKenzie retribution," countered Bare.

"She was the mother to my young grandson whose father wasn't going to be around for years and Stuart had a degree of sympathy about the beatings, he would have been ashamed of his son," explained Mary. "It must have been quite a coup for you turning a member of the family into your informant."

Bare took another sip of his drink and decided to be equally frank given the other parties involved were all now deceased.

"We did a search warrant one day at your house and I saw something between Shannon and Liam that suggested she was in fear of him so yes, there were a couple of meetings and yes, she told me about the robbery. If I had submitted the intelligence in the normal way the bosses would have not allowed us to act on it as Shannon would have been exposed as the source."

"So you just made sure you were in the right place at the right time and became an overnight hero," said Mary.

Bare gave an unapologetic shrug.

"Your boys got what they deserved and Shannon got a few years without a black eye, so is that it? Your ten minutes are up."

"I am genuinely fearful for my family. I am asking you to look at this with a fresh set of eyes, no preconceptions," she said whilst reaching into her handbag for what Bare hoped was a tissue to dab her tearing eyes.

Instead he saw she was holding a photograph of a young boy which she handed to him.

"Yes, I get you are fearful for your grandson," he said, glancing at the photograph before attempting to hand it back.

"He is my life and will always be my grandson but we are not related, he is your son," she said, finally disclosing the secret that Stuart had kept from her all that time.

CHAPTER 48

There was no guard of honour, no flag draped over the coffin and only a small number of mourners braving the cold December afternoon. Bare was disappointed but unsurprised to note he appeared to be the only serving officer there as watched the hearse arrive at the crematorium chapel. He saw Stephanie alight from the solitary black limousine that had been following the hearse and the driver hold a black umbrella over her as she did so. She was with a frail-looking older woman that he presumed was her mother and the two walked slowly into the chapel together.

The dark skies above signalled no end to the rain that had been persistently falling all day and Bare pitied the pall bearers who had to negotiate the slippery paved area at the front of the building. Once inside there was an array of empty pews available but he was politely signposted toward the front presumably to disguise the sparsity of the congregation.

The vicar officiating the service requested the mourners bow their heads for some moments of prayer or quiet contemplation and Bare chose the latter option. In truth he had done little else since his meeting with Mary McKenzie the previous day and once again his thoughts turned to his relationship with Shannon. Their first meeting had been entirely coincidental during his early police career when he had stopped her for driving along a short pedestrianised stretch of road in the town centre. Even as a rookie uniformed constable Bare had shown no interest in traffic enforcement but his Sergeant had set a monthly ticket target. He had therefore identified the most commonly committed traffic offence locality to meet his particular quota in the shortest period of time and lain in wait.

After stopping Shannon he had enjoyed her flirtatious attempts to avoid him issuing a Fixed Penalty Notice, giving as good as was receiving in terms of banter involving barely disguised innuendo. It was only when she produced her driving licence for inspection did he understand her family connections. He had made the tactical decision to replace the ticket with a 'verbal warning' on the strict understanding that she 'owed him one'. Shannon had readily agreed to the proposal which was sealed by a cheeky wink as she drove away. At that stage it had been little more than instinctive but following a couple more 'accidental' meetings he was actively on the path to cultivating her as a very useful informant, one that he had no intention of sharing despite the myriad of rules and regulations that were in place. He knew that given the identity of her husband he was playing with fire but countered that with his self-proclaimed justification of 'no risk, no reward'.

Then one evening, for the first time, Shannon had instigated contact herself. At the hastily arranged clandestine meeting he saw that her make-up was struggling to conceal a black eye and she had broken down in tears when describing her life as a perpetual victim of abuse at the hands of Liam. Bare had advised her to leave, recognising her personal safety was more important than her potential as his informant. But she had told him that deep down Liam was a good man whose behaviour was just adversely affected by those demonic twins, drink and drugs. She had also told him that although not confirmed, she believed she was pregnant.

Bare remembered putting a comforting arm around her that had unexpectedly turned into a kiss. The kiss had turned into frenzied sex and then almost as quickly into unspoken regret on both their parts. What neither knew at that point was prior to their meeting Shannon had not been pregnant but after it she certainly was.

Bare stood in silence as his fellow mourners sang The Lord Is My Shepherd whilst he continued to remember.

After three months with no contact from Shannon she again had reached out to him claiming that Liam was becoming increasingly violent and unpredictable to the extent she was fearing for her own life and that of her unborn child. Realising that she would never leave the clutches of the McKenzie clan Bare had then offered her the option of removing Liam for a period of her life. Incentivised by a Liam-free pregnancy and in the hope he would receive treatment whilst incarcerated she had then told Bare of every overheard detail about a proposed robbery, including the fact that any weapons on show would be unloaded.

As some uncle delivered a mind-numbingly boring eulogy Bare wondered whether it had ever been Shannon's intention to tell him about the paternity of Cameron. Perhaps the cryptic notes he received intermittently, including one on his wedding day, were her only means of communication given the undoubted constraints Stuart McKenzie imposed, he surmised. But the main thing Bare reflected on was the irony that he and Liam McKenzie had both unwittingly deprived each other of a child.

*

As the service concluded he met Stephanie at the chapel door as she thanked each person in turn for their attendance. She had insisted he attend the wake but Bare had no wish to return to the golf club so he made his excuses and left. As he drove back toward the police station he saw a group of children walking along the pavement in exuberant fashion having broken up from school for the Christmas holidays. He had never been very good at guessing a child's age but thought they were about the same as his son and he mouthed a silent expletive at no one in particular.

CHAPTER 49

As Avery walked down the corridor the smell reached him well in advance of the approaching people. He saw of the two it was most likely attributable to the vagrant rather than the immaculate uniformed constable escorting him. Blissfully unaware of his distinctive odour Jackanory was pleased to be leaving the building even though it had provided him with temporary warmth and a nice mug of tea whilst he had been questioned. When he suddenly saw Avery approach his demeanour changed and he furtively looked away in the vain hope of becoming invisible. His actions puzzled Avery who questioned the escorting officer as to their guest's identity.

"This is Jackanory, he's been helping DS Brady with the Vickers case," announced the uniformed constable.

"Has he now? Well very pleased to meet you, Mr Anory," said Avery, offering an outstretched hand.

"I never saw anything," he replied whilst taking Avery's hand and feeling its tight grip around his.

"Well that is a shame, we are all working hard to try and solve that one even after all this time," replied Avery. "Anyway, mustn't keep you."

Jackanory mumbled a goodbye before continuing his journey

towards the exit as Avery turned immediately into the small enquiry room where Brady was studying some papers.

"Hello Sharon, has Bare abandoned you again?" he asked.

Brady was startled, having not noticed his silent entrance into the room.

"Oh, hello sir. Yes, he has gone to DI Morton's funeral."

"Oh, of course, I would have gone myself had it not been a Superintendents' Association meeting today," he replied, providing a clear indication of his priorities. "I just had the pleasure of meeting someone you have been interviewing about Vickers."

"Oh yes, quite a character," replied Brady.

"Potential suspect?" asked Avery.

"No, nothing like that, sir, just a potential witness," she replied.

"After all these years? How did you find him?" asked Avery with growing curiosity.

"Erm, it was a bit of a long shot but we were working on the basis that Vickers was last seen in town the night before his body was found so we asked some associates where he normally parked. One of the locations he apparently used was Talbot Road."

"Bit of a run-down area I think?" replied Avery.

"Well it was back in the day, all regenerated and shiny now, but back then there was an old derelict pub there. When we were going through the files Bare remembered that Jack sometimes used to sleep in there," she explained.

"Ah, I see, any useful information?" probed Avery.

"No, he wouldn't even admit ever going in there let alone witnessing anything," explained Brady.

"Well worth a go and good thinking on Bare's part," said Avery, turning towards the door apparently satisfied.

"Yes, I think we will revisit it though, something about him, very evasive. Apparently Bare gets on with him well so may have better luck talking to him."

"Yes, they probably mix in the same social circles," laughed Avery and she laughed too as a polite acknowledgement of his humour. "I take it you will know where to find him? He has the appearance of someone who lives a rather nomadic lifestyle."

"Yes sir, that won't be a problem, he uses the Salvation Army hostel when it's really cold like now."

"Well good work, nice to know you are turning up some active lines of enquiry, let me know if you need anything," came the magnanimous departing gesture.

As he left the room Avery saw Bare walking towards it.

"How was it, Sebastian?" he enquired.

"Pretty grim," came the curt reply.

"Yes, I can imagine, still very cathartic for his wife," offered Avery.

"Yes, though there were not exactly many shoulders for her to cry on," said Bare, uncaring as to whether Avery took the remark as a personal slight.

"Well I am sure it's been a tough day and Sharon has clearly been working hard in your absence," replied Avery.

"I only went to the service, I didn't go on to the wake," replied Bare defensively, wondering whether his work ethic was being challenged.

"Oh you should have gone to that, Sebastian, I know what Jim meant to you despite everything. Anyway, I don't want you working tonight after all that so go and take Ms Brady to dinner, that's an order."

In truth Bare had no appetite to work so for once he acquiesced without argument and relayed the instruction to Brady. Avery watched them leave the building and decided he would need to re-prioritise his own evening, with Sean McKenzie gaining an unexpected stay of execution.

CHAPTER 50

The office Christmas party season made it difficult to find somewhere offering a quiet dining experience so they settled for a Chinese restaurant that appeared to be the least festively decorated compared with the neighbouring eateries.

"Do you want to talk about it?" she asked as soon as the waiter had left their table.

"Talk about what?"

"The funeral obviously, how was it?"

"It was sad on so many levels. He deserved better, Sharon," came the unexpected candid reply.

Before she was able to ask a supplementary question he found himself asking her one instead.

"Do you think it's possible the McKenzies had nothing to do with Julia's death?"

"Wow, where did that come from?" Brady managed to reply despite an inaugural bite into a prawn cracker.

"Is it possible that someone is just setting them up?" Bare persisted.

"Erm, I guess but I think it's very unlikely," she replied.

"Just humour me, tell me why, I need to hear someone else

articulate it."

She held the partially consumed appetiser in her hand as his tone suggested he was impatient for a response.

"Well you have a long history with them, there is clearly no love lost, they knew you were coming after them again, Morton gave them your address and there is corroborating DNA and other supporting evidence."

"But why not just go after me? Murdering Julia is just going to make the whole Force go after them and by bizarre coincidence it's the same night that two of their own get wiped out? It doesn't make any sense."

"You are starting to sound like their defence barrister, is it possible that you are just too emotionally involved and are overthinking things?" she replied and risked another bite as he pondered her question.

"Look, we know the gun used to shoot Liam McKenzie is linked to an OCG and the only reason we know Morton was in their pocket was because of an anonymous call. It makes no sense for the McKenzies to burn their main asset," Bare said, tapping the table with his finger to reinforce the importance of each point.

"Yes, I can see that, we don't even know that Morton was really corrupt, no irregular financials apparently."

"There doesn't have to be evidence of bribes, he could have been blackmailed," interjected Bare.

"Yes, I guess so and his suicide note sort of alluded to that," she conceded.

"I wish I knew who made that anonymous call and exactly what was said."

"You only know what you know because you have been chipping away at Avery, Jones and that poor young guy Perkins," she said and he reddened at the truthfulness of her accusation, realising he had not been as circumspect as he had thought.

"Avery has told me fuck all," he replied and by omission conceded he had received inside information from the others.

"Look, you know what it's like working on a Major Investigation, there are probably all sorts of things they are keeping tight so there is no point in speculating when you don't know all the facts. Don't assume that because Sherlock Bare isn't on the case it won't get solved."

The last part of her rebuke had descended to a whisper due to the arrival of their main course but he heard it clearly.

"For a liaison officer you are very straight talking," he observed with an accompanying smile that suggested he saw it as an endearing characteristic.

"Yeah well you already knew that, Sebastian," she retorted and mirrored his smile.

Realising she was unlikely to want further conversation concerning his dead wife Bare enquired as to the outcome of her interview with Jackanory.

"Luckily he didn't want to say much so I didn't have to endure his distinctive body odour very long, he wouldn't even admit ever sleeping in the Mariners Arms."

Bare's face betrayed the fact he was about to make a witty retort to her unintentional double entendre so she held up a prohibitive finger to stop it.

"That doesn't sound like Jack, he normally talks for England, besides, he knows we used to find him in there a lot back in the day."

"Well perhaps I am not his type, he seemed anxious to leave from the moment he sat down," she reflected.

"Well if you want a job doing well do it yourself, Sherlock," teased Bare.

"Yes, he would probably be more comfortable in the company of someone who dresses like him," she laughed whilst pointing out the sweet and sour sauce that had found its way onto the front of his jacket.

"Fuck, that's my best suit, reserved for funerals and Crown Court," he replied, furiously rubbing the spill with a napkin.

CHAPTER 51

The numbers in the queue at the Salvation Army soup kitchen had swollen due to the combination of inclement weather and the seasonal bonus of a free roast dinner. The volunteers serving the food tried to engage the recipients in some light conversation but mostly received a brief acknowledgement of thanks by those anxious to eat their first hot meal of the day. Jackanory was the notable exception as he enjoyed the human interaction almost as much as the sustenance of the turkey he was about to consume. Better still was that there was no rush to leave as he had already secured a bed for the night at the adjoining hostel, meaning he need not take part in the nightly competition to secure the deepest shop doorway.

By way of contrast Avery was not enjoying the meal but had realised a failure to eat it would probably attract unwanted attention. His hastily acquired new wardrobe that included a heavy grey trench coat and a black woollen balaclava that only partially exposed his face meant that he blended in well with his fellow diners. He had even developed a shuffling walk with a stoop which would cause a casual observer to misjudge his height by several inches. As he reluctantly ate some overcooked roast potatoes from the carefully selected vantage point he wondered whether he would get a suitable opportunity to deal with this minor inconvenience. The prospect of

Bare interviewing a witness to his spontaneous abduction all those years ago could be problematic at the very least. He was gratified to hear an announcement that the kitchen would be closing soon and hoped that it would encourage his target to move. His attention was diverted, however, upon the realisation that his previously silent neighbour was speaking to him.

"Are you eating that, mate?" said the young man, pointing a fork in the direction of the items remaining on his plastic plate.

"No, you can have it," he replied and the man needing no second invitation hurriedly took the plate and scraped the contents onto his own.

"Cheers, fella," was the gracious acknowledgement to which Avery made no reply.

In the short space of time the interaction had taken Avery had failed to notice Jackanory leave his table. A quick scan of the room revealed that he was walking toward the doorway that led to the main hostel. Relieved that he still had him in his sight Avery quickly stood up and walked toward the same door. Suddenly he felt a hand on his shoulder and swung around to discover it belonged to one of the volunteers who had served him.

"We do ask that people hand their plates back at the end," was the polite reminder that accompanied a gesture back toward his empty plate still on the table.

Frustrated about the request but unwilling to cause a scene Avery returned to the table and retrieved his plate and plastic cutlery which he quickly deposited in the appropriate container on the counter. By now he had lost sight of Jackanory so quickly walked to the door in the hope he was still visible on the other side. The door led to a small lobby that contained a stairwell leading to the accommodation area.

Avery quickly ascended the stairs but was disappointed to find an empty corridor with all the numbered bedroom doors firmly shut. Silently cursing his own lapse in concentration Avery was about to descend the stairs when one of the bedroom doors opened. He stood quietly and listened to what appeared to be a conversation between two men; one had a discernible Irish accent but the other was indistinct.

Avery tilted his head and tried to determine whether the other voice was that of his target but could not be sure so he walked slowly toward the open doorway. As he got close he saw that the departing guest from the room was an elderly man and it was him speaking as though still in his native city of Belfast. As he got closer he saw the other man was displaying a broad grin of blackened teeth that belonged to Jackanory. Avery immediately pushed in between the men so that his back was toward the Irishman and he was directly in front of Jackanory who immediately lost his smile. Avery used his gloved hand to remove a small bottle of scotch from his pocket and immediately thrust it into the hands of Jackanory who instinctively took it. Still standing on the periphery and with no view of the intruder's face the Irishman heard a shouted accusation that Jackanory had stolen the man's drink. This was immediately followed by what appeared to be a violent punch to the midriff causing his friend to slump to the floor. With that the attacker strode purposefully away leaving the Irishman to tend to his friend without fully understanding what he had witnessed. As Avery walked down the stairs he again concealed the by now bloody knife up his sleeve and was gratified nobody appeared to take much notice as he entered the by now sparsely populated dining area. Within a few minutes he was back at his car and quickly placed his outer clothing in a black bin liner before putting it in the boot.

It was several minutes before anyone responded to the blood-covered Irishman's cries for help as he cradled his stricken friend.

CHAPTER 52

'Morning Prayers' was the common term used to brief senior police managers concerning incidents of note that had happened in the preceding twenty-four hours. It was normally a tedious affair as each area's performance was measured against targets set by Chief Officers at the start of the year. Occasionally the facts and figures were relegated to second place if there had been a Major Incident overnight or at least a noteworthy occurrence. Avery anticipated that his handiwork from the previous evening would be the headline of the morning and had already decided that he would be the person to perform the media 'talking head' role. This was always a good opportunity for self-promotion and he knew that his public reassurance message would play well in the eyes of the Police and Crime Commissioner.

Sure enough when all the morning coffees had been poured, the nominated briefing officer, a studious crime analyst, started his presentation with a report of a serious incident at the Salvation Army hostel. He described how officers had responded to a reported disturbance between residents and discovered that a local well-known character had been stabbed. The offender was unknown at this stage but was believed to be a rough sleeper.

Avery saw that the incident barely generated a flicker of interest amongst his fellow managers and decided to score a few points with an early seizure of the moral high ground.

"Ladies and gentlemen, I realise the victim and offender here may come from a particular socio-economic group but frankly I am appalled by the levels of indifference being displayed here. We are being briefed about a murder on our patch with an offender still at large so please show some professional courtesy and respect."

The room fell silent and Avery enjoyed looking at the sea of embarrassed faces around him as he gestured for the briefing to continue.

The analyst cleared his throat and checked his notes before reluctantly realising it fell to him to correct the Detective Superintendent who was now staring directly at him.

"Erm, it wasn't a murder, sir, the victim is in hospital as a result of the attack but is still alive."

Avery took a moment to maintain his composure as a consequence of the unexpected update. He noted that a couple of people in the room even had the temerity to smile at his expense but he chose not to challenge them.

"Well that is obviously good news and will teach me not to make assumptions," he said with more meaning than the room could possibly know.

The rest of the briefing seemed to take an eternity as it moved onto other topics leaving Avery with a growing uneasiness about his potential vulnerability. He had been certain that the angle and force of his attack had been sufficient to produce a fatal result and was confounded that Jackanory had apparently survived. As soon as he could without drawing undue attention he managed to extradite himself from the room and sought out the team investigating the stabbing. He found them being briefed by a young Detective Inspector who had been drafted in to replace Morton. He had no prior knowledge of the officer but had been unimpressed during an initial meet and greet a couple of days earlier.

The Detective Inspector stopped the briefing upon seeing Avery walk into the room but the senior officer requested that he carry on, assuming the role of an interested spectator. Avery guessed he had walked in at the very end of the briefing as the Detective Inspector merely summarised the priority lines of enquiry before dismissing the freshly assembled team of detectives assigned to the case. After waiting patiently for the room to clear Avery asked the DI for his assessment of the investigation. Eager to impress his new boss, DI Backhouse diligently offered his policy file for perusal.

"No, I am sure that's all very detailed and accurate, I just want an overview," said Avery, handing the unopened file back.

"Well I am not sure how much you know, sir, but our victim appears to have been in dispute with an as yet unknown person who had accused him of stealing some alcohol. There was an altercation and the victim was stabbed in the stomach, very lucky to survive by all accounts. We have one witness, an intoxicated Irishman who we are waiting to properly interview once he is fully sober, which could be around Tuesday next week by all accounts."

Avery ignored the ill-judged attempt at humour and asked what information had been gleaned from the victim.

"Nothing as yet, I am afraid, sir, he is in intensive care and they have induced a coma. To be honest I think it's 50/50 whether he survives."

"Is that what the hospital have told us or are you drawing on a medical background?" asked Avery whilst perusing the crime scene photographs displayed on a notice board.

"Erm, just going on what was overheard at the hospital by one of the uniform lads," conceded Backhouse with growing concern about his obvious failure to endear himself to Avery.

"Okay, keep me updated, the Chief will be looking for a quick result on this one," instructed Avery before leaving the room.

Backhouse was still reeling from the encounter when he was joined by two more guests.

"Hi Guv'nor, DS Seb Bare and DS Sharon Brady," said the man by way on introduction as he extended his arm for a handshake.

"Hi, Mike Backhouse," came the reply as he greeted both officers. "Is Mr Avery always so brusque or was it just me?" was his supplementary question that instantly made Bare smile.

"Yes, he's a bit uptight, typical high flyer," was Bare's response that earned a reproachful look from Brady.

"I don't know if you have been made aware, sir, but I interviewed the victim yesterday in connection with a cold case that Seb and I are working on," said Brady, eager to ensure a professional footing was established.

"Yes, you have saved me a trip to come and see you as one of the enquiry team mentioned Jack was here yesterday. I am afraid he may not be of much use to you anymore as a witness, bad way apparently," replied Backhouse.

"To be honest he wasn't much use to us yesterday but we were intending to reinterview him," explained Brady.

"Can you tell us what happened? I have known Jack for a long time and he has never been involved in a fight before, bit of a local character, that's all," asked Bare as he too was drawn to the displayed crime scene photographs.

"Well it looks like Jack stole a bottle of whisky off another street drinker and got stabbed for his troubles," explained Backhouse.

"That doesn't sound like him," remarked Bare as he studied the photographs of blood splatters in a doorway that identified the point of the attack.

"Well that's all we have managed to get from our witness at the moment together with a sketchy description of the offender. Mr Avery has suggested he wants a quick result too which may be a challenge," said Backhouse, wondering if the remainder of his career was dependant on the outcome.

"Is this the whisky that Jack allegedly stole?" asked Bare, pointing to a photograph of a discarded bottle close to the ominously large pool of blood.

"It must be as it was the only one recovered from his room, we are waiting for forensics on it," replied Backhouse.

"Well whatever the motive was it wasn't theft. Jack would never touch this cheap shit," said Bare.

"Oh he was a discerning street drinker, was he?" laughed Backhouse.

"Yes, he is," said Bare, correcting the Inspector's use of the past tense.

CHAPTER 53

"Well that was fun, alienating another supervisory officer," said Brady as she struggled to keep up with Bare's strides along the corridor.

"Sanctimonious prick," was Bare's immediate retort.

"Your interpersonal skills are really improving."

"Well what do you expect? He is totally out of his depth, no wonder Avery gave him a hard time," said Bare, struggling to control his anger at the way the meeting two minutes earlier had deteriorated so quickly.

"You didn't really give him a chance. No DI is going to welcome some bolshy Sergeant telling him how to do his job," she said with a calming touch on his arm.

Bare was about to challenge her label of him but then elected not to for fear of being distracted. As the pair returned to their own office he began searching through a pile of papers on his desk without providing any form of commentary to the watching Brady. When she could no longer endure his obvious growing frustration she enquired what he was searching for. Instead of providing a direct answer he asked a question to her as he continued on his quest.

"What if Morton wasn't the only leak here?"

She was unsure whether the question had intended to be rhetorical as Bare didn't appear to be waiting for an answer but she responded anyway.

"Are you saying that the stabbing last night is connected to something else?"

This time he did answer her question as he concentrated on the witness statement he had been searching for.

"The last sighting of Vickers was him walking alone towards Talbot Road, we know that he habitually parked his car there and as soon as we dig up a witness who might have seen him the same witness gets randomly attacked and left for dead. That's a hell of a coincidence, what if someone here is feeding information to whoever killed Vickers?"

Brady took a moment to process the information but was clearly struggling to arrive at the same conclusion as Bare.

"That's a lot of 'what ifs' and remember Jackanory denied seeing Vickers or even ever dossing at the Mariners Arms," she reminded her colleague.

"Yes, that's the bit I am really struggling with. Jack is an old rogue but he would have no reason to lie about something that we know to be true, he even showed me around the place one night," replied Bare, smiling at the memory, "and like I said to Hercule Poirot, Jack is not a thief and he would certainly never nick a budget brand of scotch."

"I hope the next part of your theory is not going to link the McKenzies into all this," said Brady, trying to second guess her partner's ulterior motive.

In truth Bare was going to make no such accusation although there was a probable connection with all local minor drug suppliers like Vickers and the sophisticated network that Stuart McKenzie ran.

The mention of the family name did, however, cause him to check his watch and note that it was still another two hours before he was due to meet Mary again. His mind replayed aspects of their last meeting as it had done pretty much continuously since she had left him shellshocked in his apartment. No matter how many other scenarios he considered he could not escape the fact that he was certain she had been truthful about the parentage of Cameron and he now really wanted to meet his son.

Brady observed Bare retreat into his own private thoughts and realised he remained the closed book she had struggled to read all those years ago. The only difference about this modern version was that the previous impervious cover was no longer fully intact, allowing her to see some small fragments of uncertainty and vulnerability beneath. She silently rebuked herself for noticing, as she realised it signalled her attraction to this bloody man was beginning to grow again.

"No, I can't think of an obvious link," Bare belatedly replied, "which is just as well as I wouldn't be allowed to continue on the case."

"Okay, so what do we do now?" she asked, hoping he had not noticed the growing blush that had involuntarily accompanied her moment of self-realisation.

"I think we need a coffee fix," he replied and she was grateful to be left alone as he disappeared toward the canteen.

CHAPTER 54

Avery's irritation concerning Jackanory's stubborn determination to remain alive was exacerbated further by the lack of an opportunity to dispatch Sean McKenzie as efficiently as his late brother. The frustration of having untidy loose ends was made worse by ACC West's growing appetite for regular updates about the 'alarming escalation' of violent crime on Avery's patch. He sensed that his supervisor was buckling under the political pressure to steady the ship and he was being set up as the fall guy. The irony that it was his actions that had caused the sharp spike in unfavourable performance figures completely bypassed him as he sullenly listened to the condescending lecture being delivered to him via a speaker phone. He let West finish the diatribe and deliberately paused before responding. He was skilled enough to provide the platitudes needed and of course took the time to thank the senior officer for his unwavering support before the call ended.

In the secretary's office outside Ann saw the light on her switchboard phone extinguish so told Bare that Mr Avery now appeared to be free. He knocked on the door by way of introduction and immediately entered to find Avery leaning back in his chair as though in a state of reflection.

"Sorry to interrupt, was wondering if I could have a quick word."

Avery looked up and was momentarily puzzled at the sudden appearance of Bare holding two takeaway coffee cups.

"Always got time for you, Sebastian, especially as you have come bearing a drink."

"Well the canteen was on the way," said Bare, handing over the latte he had purchased for Brady.

"What can I do for you?" asked Avery.

"I think I need to be on the stabbing investigation from last night, the victim is a witness in our case and DI Backhouse could do with a hand," explained Bare.

"And is that his view or yours?" said Avery.

Bare took a sip of his own coffee as he tried to think of a way of masking the obvious transparency of his request. The molten hot contents of the insulated cup burnt his tongue and instead of a considered comment he found himself instinctively providing a spluttered expletive.

"From what I understand DI Backhouse has adequate resources to investigate the matter which amounts to a dispute between two of our charming knights of the road," continued Avery as Bare made some futile efforts to wipe away some coffee splatter from his trouser leg.

"Well that may be the case but I don't think we should discount the possibility that the attack is connected to our case, we were about to establish whether Jack was a key witness and then out of the blue he gets stabbed," said Bare, deciding to ignore the stains and focus on his explanation to Avery.

"What do you mean 'a key witness'?" asked Avery, leaning forward with genuine interest.

"Well I think that Vickers parked his car that night in Talbot Road and Jack was dossing in the pub that used to be there, he would have seen whether our victim was with someone," said Bare, encouraged that he was being given an opportunity to present his case.

"But I thought DS Brady had already interviewed your witness and that he had provided a negative statement?" said Avery.

Bare suppressed his surprise that Avery was better briefed than he had expected and continued to reassert his belief that Jack was a key witness.

"Sharon doesn't know him and for whatever reason I think he lied to her but I am confident he will tell me the truth as we go back a way."

"Okay but that doesn't explain why you want to join DI Backhouse's team, why do you think the attack is linked to your investigation, Sebastian?"

"Call it an instinct but I told you before that there could be a leak at the nick and perhaps it wasn't entirely plugged by the death of Jim Morton," said Bare with a growing belief he was successfully addressing the scepticism of his boss.

Avery again leaned back in his chair in apparent deep consideration before delivering his verdict.

"Tell you what, Sebastian, I will tell DI Backhouse to keep you in the loop but I think you should continue your own investigation for now. But thank you for the coffee," smiled Avery as he raised the cup in acknowledgment of the gift and also as an indication the meeting had concluded.

Bare knew there was little to be gained from appealing the decision so decided to graciously withdraw.

"Okay, boss," he said and walked toward the door. As he opened it he turned back towards Avery who was already busying himself with another matter selected from his 'in-tray'.

"Oh, there was one other thing," said Bare, causing Avery to sigh at the further interruption of his work. "Did you ever get questioned about the Vickers murder?"

Avery greeted the question with a puzzled expression.

"It was just I went through all the old duty books and you were shown as doing foot patrol the night he went missing," said Bare.

"Was I really? Blimey that's going back a few years, must have been just before I transferred. I have a vague recollection of the case but no, I don't think the original enquiry team specifically spoke to me," replied Avery.

"Was just a thought, I guess you would have told them at the time if you had seen anything of interest," said Bare before closing the door en route to the canteen to buy Brady another coffee.

CHAPTER 55

Mary McKenzie nervously awaited Bare's arrival as she watched the endless waves crash onto the deserted beach. The inshore wind made the December afternoon feel even colder and she sank her hands deep in her coat pockets. She regretted her lapse in concentration which meant her gloves were still in her car and contemplated returning for them when she saw him walking toward her. His languid gait provided no clue as to his mood but she hoped that the time lapse since their last meeting would have had a calming effect on him.

As he got closer he appeared to scan their immediate surroundings and she guessed he was assessing his potential vulnerability to an ambush. When she looked closer she spotted the momentary expression of disappointment that crossed his face and she understood the reason for his surveillance.

"He is at school, he wanted to see his friends before they broke up for Christmas," was her greeting and answer to his unasked question.

"Does he like school?" Bare asked and she was reassured by his soft tone.

"As much as most boys his age but he is a clever lad," she replied.

"How is he coping without his mum and...?" asked Bare, unsure as to how to refer to Liam McKenzie.

"Kids are very resilient. Of course he misses his mum but in truth he was only just getting to know his dad, I mean Liam," she answered, determined to keep her own emotions in check.

"I didn't know if you would bring him, I mean obviously not to tell him but just, well, you know," said Bare, unable to articulate his thoughts.

"Why, have you got a wee DNA kit in your pocket?" she said, fixing him with a stare that made him protest his innocence.

"No, there's no need for that, I know there is no reason for you to have invented something about your grandson who you are clearly very close to."

His affirmation caused her to bite her lip to once again prevent vocalisation of her grief and she knew she had to engage her business mode.

"So if you believe that do you also believe my boys had nothing to do with your wife's death?"

Bare looked at the woman and saw she was desperately seeking some reassurance from him.

"To be honest I don't know what to believe, there has been so much that has happened that I am struggling to provide a narrative that explains it all," was his honest if qualified response.

There was a pause as she waited for amplification but when none came she pressed him as expertly as any defence barrister he had formerly encountered.

"So that at least suggests you now have considerable doubts about my boys?"

Bare smiled as he remembered the ferocity his own mother had displayed when he was a child whilst defending him from third-party accusations of wrongdoing. He also recalled that despite the tenacity of her rebuttals he was on the majority of occasions guilty as charged.

"Let's say I now have more of an open mind," he conceded.

Realising it was unlikely she would gain further ground Mary changed her tact and asked a question that she felt would provide an insight into Bare's character.

"Tell me, Sebastian, why are you so personally invested in bringing my family down?"

Bare was going to deny the accusation but felt that for once he was with someone who probably deserved to know the ridiculous truth.

"Because when I was a very young-in-service constable in uniform something happened between me and Liam," he replied. "I had only just started doing solo foot patrol and was walking through the town one evening. It was a Saturday and summertime, there were so many people about, tourists and locals, and I was feeling very self-conscious in my uniform. I remember walking past a pub and there were loads of people drinking outside. A police officer on lone patrol is always going to be the target of some drunken comments and they never really bothered me but what I wasn't expecting was someone to knock my helmet off. The shock of it somehow made me lose my balance and I fell onto a table that was full of drinks. The crash was spectacular and I ended up sitting amongst the debris with my uniform soaked in stale beer. I was so angry and embarrassed but the laughter and cheering was deafening. I had no way of knowing who had caused it but when I looked up at the crowd of faces I knew for certain that the young lad in the middle was responsible. You see it was the subtle wink he gave me as he helped me to my feet, knowing I could do absolutely nothing about it. After that I made a point of finding out all about Liam McKenzie and so it all began."

"And that's why you winked at him after he was sentenced in Court, all of this because he knocked your bloody helmet off." Mary shook her head in disbelief.

"We were both young bucks and stupid," was Bare's only muted response.

"I am not sure you deserve to meet your son," she replied.

"Well that's up to you, have a think about it," said Bare.

"It's a bit late for that," she said, waving to her friend walking towards them with Cameron who had just been collected from school on her behalf.

Upon seeing his grandmother the boy left his escort and ran excitedly towards her seemingly ignoring the presence of the male stranger in her company. After the friend departed leaving the three of them on the otherwise deserted seafront, Mary introduced them.

"Cameron, this is one of the policemen that's finding out what happened to your mum and dad."

"Hello," replied the boy, holding out his hand as his late grandfather had taught him. "When I grow up I want to be a policeman."

Bare smiled as he shook the remarkably polite boy's hand, still shocked by the meeting that Mary had clearly prearranged.

"Can I ask you a question?" said Cameron.

"Of course you can," replied Bare.

"I was watching a police programme on the television and is it right that if you are fighting with a criminal you have to wait for him to hit you first before you are allowed to hit him back? Because that means the policeman is always going to get hurt and that doesn't seem fair."

Bare laughed at the random question but saw that the boy was looking at him earnestly with the full expectation of a considered reply.

"Well if you are absolutely sure the criminal is going to hurt you sometimes you are allowed to push him away first and then call on your radio for help, but don't worry, you will get trained after you join up."

The father, son and grandmother spoke for a few more minutes before the rain started and they parted. As they separated Bare mouthed a silent 'thank you' to Mary but she made no comment; her face indicated she was still uncertain as to whether the meeting had been a good idea. He watched them walk hurriedly away toward the clifftop car park, hand in hand and with Cameron no doubt telling her excitedly about his last day at school. Not until they were out of sight did Bare walk slowly towards his own car with no plan in his mind beyond putting one foot in front of another.

CHAPTER 56

Avery hated loose ends and recognised the continuous distraction of them sometimes caused him to lose focus. His mind needed to be like his desk, tidy and organised, so that he could attend to the in-tray methodically and efficiently. Sean McKenzie and Jackanory were like irritating coffee stains on his otherwise immaculate leather-bound blotter and he was struggling to contain the irrational rage their presence was causing.

He closed his eyes to aid concentration and the re-establishment of calm rational thought. The prognosis for the comatose patient was that the problem may well resolve itself without the need for further intervention so that was a secondary priority. *Good, this is better, clearer analysis,* he thought to himself. So by a process of elimination he knew he needed to concentrate on McKenzie and that, he reassured himself, would restore some equilibrium.

The problem was McKenzie was understandably laying low and no doubt close to the bosom of his precious family so he had to devise a plan to remove the safety net. Anyone observing Avery would have assumed he was replaying a tennis match in his mind as his head tilted from one side to another but it was just his way of developing an idea and assessing its strengths and weaknesses. When his eyes opened it meant that he had finished the threat assessment stage and was ready to move on to implementation. Within a few seconds of opening his eyes he picked up his phone and requested DCI Jones attend his office as soon as possible.

Gareth Jones gathered up his policy files and left the Major Incident room with a weary resignation having received the call. He had never been required to report to a senior officer with the regularity that Avery had demanded and wondered whether it signalled a significant doubt in his ability. He consoled himself in the knowledge that other Senior Investigating Officers were experiencing the same levels of scrutiny and concluded that it probably spoke volumes about their esteemed leader's own insecurities. Nevertheless, this would be the second required update in less than six hours and Jones wondered what possible new information he was expected to bring to the table.

Avery greeted his arrival with a lack of the normal pleasantries social etiquette dictated, signalling to Jones there was urgent business to be discussed.

"I have received another anonymous call, obviously I can't be certain but it sounded like the same person who provided the information about Morton," the senior officer announced.

Jones was unsure whether the pause that followed Avery's revelation was there to be filled by him or whether it was just whilst notes were being examined to relay the exact information that had been freshly received. Avery quickly answered the question by reading aloud the contemporaneous notes he had presumably recorded upon receipt of the call.

"The team who killed Liam McKenzie are actively seeking his brother."

"Well, we have provided Sean McKenzie with appropriate advice as per the manual of guidance. I believe he is keeping his head down and obviously he remains a strong suspect concerning Julia Bare so we are keeping tabs," offered Jones.

"Okay, obviously I will write up the intelligence report and submit it but I just wanted to make sure you were aware as ultimately it's your head on the block in terms of duty of care etcetera," said Avery, matter-of-factly.

"Well there is not much else we can do other than perhaps tell him we have been made aware of a specific threat against him now," said Jones, feeling uncomfortable with Avery's less than subtle transference of responsibility.

"Fine, I will rely on your professional judgement, Gareth, do an appropriate entry in your policy file and I will countersign it."

With that, Avery took some unrelated papers from his desk, signalling that from his perspective the meeting was at an end. Jones hesitated as it was unusual for Avery not to impart some advice or strategic direction, leaving him to wonder whether he needed to do something else in order to safeguard himself from future scrutiny.

"I suppose we could move him to a safe house," he offered.

"Yes, good idea, Gareth, but don't go overboard on an escort, we still can't be sure there are no leaks," said Avery.

"One AFO (Authorised Firearms Officer) would be OK, I can use DC Perkins from the enquiry team to keep it tight, he got his ticket last year," said Jones, confident that his problem-solving skills were working well in front of his boss.

"Yes, whatever, I don't need to know the detail. Well done, Gareth," said the expert puppeteer. "Just make sure he uses the covert people carrier, we don't want there to be any chance of McKenzie being seen."

CHAPTER 57

The unfamiliar weight of the Glock 17 in his covert harness made Perkins nervous as he left Avery's office. Although fully trained he was a relatively inexperienced firearms officer and this was the first time he had been asked to 'babysit' a vulnerable person. The exact location of the 'safe house' was a closely guarded secret that would only be revealed to him by someone in the Witness Protection Unit once he had confirmed he had collected McKenzie, whom he would refer to as Oscar One. As he rounded the corridor corner he literally walked into Sebastian Bare, causing them both to mutually apologise. Bare introduced him to DS Sharon Brady who had narrowly avoided the collision as a result of swift evasive action on her part.

"So where you off to in such a hurry?" enquired Bare.

The young officer was conscious of his own rapid blush as he tried to deflect the question with a blasé reply about being sent on a donut run by the enquiry team.

"Yes, that can be quite a dangerous task," said Bare, pointing to the concealed weapon he had felt as the two came together.

"Shit, look am sworn to secrecy, Sarge, and I am especially not supposed to talk to you about it," said the by now scarlet junior officer.

Bare held up his palms in a placatory gesture and reassured him he didn't 'need to know' but wished the officer good luck before they parted. After the relieved Perkins had hurried away Brady congratulated her partner on his self-restraint.

"Well I could hardly ask him with you standing there," he replied, leaving her to wonder how true that comment was.

When Perkins reached the underground secure parking area he was relieved to see the little-used dark blue people carrier with its dark tinted windows had been left in an accessible parking space. He made a cursory inspection of the exterior, a familiar routine so as not to be held responsible for someone else's unreported damage, before getting into the vehicle and performing a radio check. Satisfied everything was in order he set off in order to pick up the charming Oscar One whom he hoped wouldn't be too unbearable in his company.

As Bare and Brady entered the police canteen the vibration in his pocket alerted him to the fact that someone was attempting to call him. A surreptitious check of the caller display informed him as to the caller's number which had become recently familiar to him and he excused himself from Brady to take the call in a quiet corner.

He listened as a concerned Mary McKenzie explained the police wanted to take her son into protective custody for a short period time whilst they assessed a threat made against him. Bare looked across at Brady who was theatrically miming 'tea or coffee' and saw her infuriation as he pretended not to understand. He then returned his attention to the call and realised why Perkins had been so circumspect with him. After reassuring Mary that it was standard procedure and 'not to worry' he added that she should tell Sean to be on his best behaviour as the officer assigned to him was one of the best he had worked with. She thanked him and apologised for contacting him which made him think about the strange dynamic that was developing between them. He then quickly terminated the call as he saw Brady approach with two cups of tea in her hands.

"Oh, I wanted coffee," he said but she knew it was a deliberate tease on his part so made no direct comment in response.

The two sat down at a free table and she was unable to resist any longer.

"So which one of the harem was that?" she asked.

"Actually it was an old mate from the past who was asking after my welfare, given the fact my wife recently died," he replied.

"Yeah right," was the immediate retort. She knew him well enough to spot a lie as transparent as his earlier claim for a coffee had been.

"Why, would you be jealous if it had been a woman?" he asked and was immediately surprised that an involuntary flick of her hair told him that she most definitely would.

CHAPTER 58

Mary viewed the officer with some suspicion, wondering whether someone younger than her son could be trusted with the responsibility of keeping him safe. She did, however, trust Bare's glowing endorsement and had indeed told Sean to be a respectful companion. For his part Perkins had approached the task with diligent professionalism even though the role had little appeal for him and represented an abstraction from the detective role where he was starting to flourish. He consoled himself with the fact that a prolonged period of time in the company of the notorious Sean McKenzie would hopefully provide a valuable insight into the criminal mind. As he observed the said criminal trudge toward him like a sullen teenager he started to realise that his hope was probably on the optimistic side. This was further confirmed when after a brief discussion with his mother, Sean huffed loudly and returned to the house evidently to collect some forgotten personal item. When he returned with a freshly acquired overnight bag over his shoulder, Perkins took the opportunity to introduce himself and set out the ground rules.

When he heard this meant relinquishing his brand new mobile phone to avoid any potential compromise Sean looked at his mother signalling this was to be his excuse for a cessation of the brief co-operation with the police he had endured. Mary recognised the facial expression before it became vocal and reasserted her strong view these measures were necessary for his safety. Reluctantly he handed over his phone to her, realising she was wearing her non-negotiation expression.

"Right, we really need to make a move. Just to remind you there can be no direct contact with Sean whilst he is with us but you have the witness protection number, Mrs McKenzie," said Perkins as he opened the rear passenger door for Oscar One.

"I need you to take Cameron too," said Mary, beckoning over the eight-year-old boy who had been patiently waiting in the entrance hall with his rucksack by his side and football in his hands.

"No, sorry, the threat at this stage just relates to Sean as it was explained on the phone earlier," said Perkins as the boy approached with the same sullen look of his uncle.

"Well I have just spoken to your witness protection people and have told them if there is a threat to my family you should be protecting them both."

"Aye, and you too, Ma," called out Sean from within the vehicle.

Mary ignored her son's comment and directed her firm gaze at Perkins.

"I have some extended family arriving later from Glasgow so I will be fine but please take my boys, Mr Perkins," she implored.

Irritated that he was already falling behind schedule Perkins reached for his encrypted radio that provided contact with the Witness Protection Co-ordinator but before he could transmit he received an incoming message. He walked away a few paces to ensure the transmission could not be overheard before returning a short time later and ushering Oscar Two into the vehicle alongside his uncle.

"Thank you, son, look after them both," she said, using both her hands to momentarily hold his as if to emphasise her plea.

"They will both be fine and hopefully home sooner rather than later," he replied before quickly getting into the vehicle and entering the address he had just been provided into the vehicle's satellite navigation system. He saw that their destination was less than two hours away and was pleased to have some local knowledge regarding the whereabouts of the hastily arranged safe house.

As he pulled onto the main road close to the McKenzie residence Perkins scanned the traffic for any potential unwanted observers. Although nothing aroused his suspicion he nevertheless took some standard anti-surveillance measures until he was completely confident that no one was following. During the journey any insight into the criminal mind was severely hindered by the loud snores of Sean McKenzie who was clearly not as stressed about the covert operation as his mother. Therefore conversation was limited to an exchange with Cameron regarding the latter's ambition to become a police officer as he had been recently reassured it was okay to make a pre-emptive strike on a 'baddie'. Anxious not to perpetuate the myth of police brutality Perkins took his time to explain the restrictions around 'use of force' but sensed the unknown conveyor of the original message had made far more of an impression than he was attempting. When that topic was exhausted the two found more common ground with their choice of football allegiances which made the journey pass quicker.

Avery smiled as he watched the screen of his mobile phone showing the accurate location of the tracking device he had placed under the rear wheel arch of the vehicle earlier that day. After the early obvious anti-surveillance measures had made the destination unclear it now appeared to be heading toward a rural coastal region that he recognised with fondness from his childhood.

CHAPTER 59

It took a moment for Bare to remember who Robin was when she telephoned leading to an awkward laugh at both ends of the conversation. This had been their first contact since Bare had been abruptly recalled from London and she apologised profusely for the inappropriate email she had sent before becoming aware of the tragedy that had surrounded him.

Bare told her she had no reason to apologise and only the presence of Brady nearby stopped a resumption of the flirting they had enjoyed over dinner.

"Anyways I just wanted to tell you that I concluded all the financial analysis of the McKenzies and passed it all down to your investigation team," she said, professional composure regained given Bare's businesslike tone.

"Thanks, that's great Robin, obviously I am not on the team anymore but I know they have made good use of it," he replied, wondering whether the call had just been an excuse to re-establish contact.

"Well there's a little more," she said. "Once the gun that was used to kill Shannon McKenzie was traced back to one of our Organised Crime Groups I was asked to see if there were any links between them and the McKenzies."

"And you have found something?" asked Bare with growing curiosity.

"Erm, not exactly, in fact there is not a single attributable intelligence link between the two groups whatsoever which is very strange if there had been a growing turf war between them."

"Okay, well perhaps it was something else, maybe Stuart McKenzie shagged one of their grandmothers and left without paying the bill," he speculated and the comment caused Brady to raise her eyebrows in puzzlement.

"Nope, I trawled every intelligence database and input all the names from your end to try and find an overlap but there is no common link, well except one quirky one."

"And by quirky you mean…?"

"Well it is probably nothing but I didn't want not to mention it and then I didn't know who I should mention it to or in what format," said Robin with increasing regret that she had made the call.

"Robin, it's fine, just tell me and I will tell you what you should do, there is obviously something that caused you to call."

"It's Paul Avery," she said flatly. "He is the only link between the two Organised Crime Groups."

"OK, well I guess that is kind of obvious as he worked in the Met and now back here so may have had some contact with both at some point in his career," said Bare, struggling to hide the disappointment in his voice.

"No, it's more than that, you see he never had any obvious dealings with our group, he never arrested them or even submitted any intelligence reports but I just happened across his scrawl of a signature on a single document, an exhibit schedule from a search warrant when an absolute shedload of firearms were seized including ones very similar to the one used in the McKenzie shooting. It's bizarre because had I not worked for him I would have never been able to decipher the signature but I recognised it. As I said it's probably absolutely nothing but I just wanted to…"

"It's fine, I absolutely understand and you did the right thing, Robin. Leave it with me, OK?" said Bare.

The two exchanged a few more pleasantries and wished each other a pleasant Christmas, causing Robin to once again apologise for being insensitive at the very mention of family before the call was concluded with a mutual promise to catch up in the New Year which both in reality knew to be unlikely.

Brady saw that Bare was in a contemplative state when the call finished but she had overheard enough of it to be intrigued as to the finer detail.

"Another admirer?" she asked, hoping her enquiry would be construed as playful.

"It was the Met analyst who did some work on the McKenzie finances, I think she was casting some aspersions on the integrity of the 'Special One'," he replied, still trying to compute the information Robin had passed to him.

"Oh, do tell, love a bit of gossip," she replied but then understood in an instance that her jocular encouragement was misplaced. "Seb, what do you mean?" she added with appropriate gravitas in her tone.

"I'm not sure, it's probably nothing, but I think I want to look him in the eyes when I ask him about it," concluded Bare, already walking toward the door.

"Seb, don't you think we should discuss…" She realised the

futility of completing her sentence as he was already out of the office and the sudden ring of the desk phone prevented any notion of her pursuing him.

During the short journey to Avery's office Bare formulated a plan that basically amounted to instigating a conversation and then improvising based on any reactions it caused. It wasn't the greatest example of strategic thinking but it was a tried and tested weapon from his personal arsenal of interview techniques. An essential component of the plan was, however, the presence of Avery and his absence left him without an immediate contingency.

"He's taken the afternoon off, is there anything I can do for you?" Ann asked with only a slight raise of an eyebrow to emphasise the innuendo in her comment.

"Not today sadly," he replied.

"Story of my life," she said aloud but he had already left with the speed of a man on a mission.

CHAPTER 60

After Perkins had confirmed the safe arrival of Oscar One and Two with a short message to the Protection Unit command, he took a deep breath of the invigorating sea air before recovering the door key from the coded box. The cottage was a small unremarkable building that was assumed by locals to be one of many holiday lets in the area. Whilst there were no immediate neighbours the property was close enough to others so as not be conspicuous through its isolation. It also provided good natural surveillance of any persons approaching it whether by foot or vehicle so ticked all the 'safe house' boxes. The inside was furnished with functional rather than stylish fixtures and fittings which caused Sean McKenzie's face to display a look of barely disguised disgust at the spartan nature of his new surroundings. By contrast Cameron was warming to the adventure and the sight of a goal net in the rear garden added to his delight.

"Make yourselves comfortable," urged Perkins who was gratified that whoever had prepared the cottage had remembered to switch on the heating system. "Hopefully we won't be here too long," he added whilst checking the provisions in the freshly stocked fridge and cupboards.

"How long is normal?" asked McKenzie.

"Well this is just a temporary place, it buys us a bit of thinking time so the threat can be properly assessed," explained Perkins who saw that McKenzie was expecting a more numeric answer so added, "typically no more than twenty-four hours. If the threat is considered serious enough you and your family may be offered something more permanent subject to you co-operating."

"We don't need anything permanent, we just need your lot to do your job and catch whoever is taking us on, or better still just tell us their names and my family will sort it themselves," snarled McKenzie with only the remembered promise to his mother preventing the observation becoming more vitriolic.

"Well we take our duty of care very seriously for whoever is under threat," replied Perkins calmly, keen not inflame the situation in front of the ever widening eyes of Cameron.

"Can I go outside and play football, Uncle Sean?" asked his nephew, the football already in his hand in expectation of an affirmative answer.

McKenzie displayed his uncertainty about his situation by looking to Perkins for guidance which both surprised and pleased the police officer in equal measure. In order to establish some rapport with the man he constructed an answer to satisfy both McKenzie and his nephew.

"You can play outside if it's okay with your uncle but you must keep to the back garden so come and get one of us if the ball goes over the fence, deal?"

"Deal," he replied solemnly as he took the offer on an outstretched hand to make the contract binding.

Any thoughts that the two men left inside the cottage would use the opportunity to learn more about each other were quickly dashed as McKenzie declared he was going for a sleep leaving Perkins to feel like the anxious babysitter as he made regular observations through the rear window. Whilst he understood the rationale for making this a solo assignment he could not help wishing he had a colleague with him to share the burden.

Unbeknown to Perkins a colleague was less than ten miles away driving the rental car around the often challenging bends of the coastal road. Avery periodically checked the tracker display laying on the otherwise unoccupied front passenger seat of the car and saw that the target device had now been static for nearly an hour. It was strange that the safe house was clearly in an area that he knew well from his childhood and he hoped that the familiarity of his surroundings would compensate for the relative hasty preparation of his plan. His own car would have been collected by now from outside his home address and would be travelling back to the garage from where he had purchased it for a full valet. The unsuspecting driver would be helpfully driving past a number of ANPR cameras that would record the route and be corroborated by any cell site analysis of his mobile phone that he had left on silent mode in the glove compartment. He saw no reason why he would ever need an alibi but whilst he was en route to kill Sean McKenzie modern technology was helpfully providing him with one.

Within a few minutes he was close enough to guess the safe house was one of a few spaced out properties that led into the picturesque village of Holstead. During the summer tourists would cause the population to swell exponentially and it would be common to sit in a queue of slow-moving traffic that infuriated the locals every year. At this time of year, however, the traffic was sparse and he had not seen any life for miles save for some livestock that appeared to be huddled together for protection from the wind sweeping in from the sea. He drove past a number of different properties, slowing down but not so much as to be conspicuous and saw the familiar people carrier parked on a driveway. The only thing that made the cottage look different from others he had passed was the lack of Christmas decorations that adorned more festive neighbouring properties. He drove about another half a mile before finding a convenient place to turn around and retrace his route back to the 'safe' house that was about to become anything but.

CHAPTER 61

DC Perkins completed his hourly radio status update whilst marvelling at the young boy's seemingly endless appetite to kick a football into an unguarded goal and then wheel away mimicking the celebration of a world cup winner. His attention then switched to the front window as he saw a dark-coloured saloon car park at the front of the property. Instinctively he picked up his radio only to lower it again as he recognised the sole occupant of the car walking briskly down the path toward the front door. He opened the door before Avery had a chance to knock on it and politely stood aside to allow the senior officer quick access. After checking there were to be no other unexpected visitors he closed the door and greeted his boss.

"I wasn't expecting to see you here, sir, is everything okay?" said Perkins, struggling to recall the protocols that would allow such a visit.

"No, not really, there is a possibility that this location has been compromised so I have been asked to come and do a personal assessment. Is your Subject safe?" said Avery briskly.

"Yes, he is having a sleep upstairs, what do you mean 'compromised', sir? I have just checked in with Witness Protection," said Perkins, increasingly worried that he had omitted to do something expected of him.

"It's a potential anti-corruption matter. Have you discussed this operation with DS Bare?" said Avery.

Perkins gulped as he recalled the brief encounter with Sebastian Bare in the police station corridor earlier that day before spluttering, "No sir, the only persons I have spoken to apart from yourself is DCI Jones and the Witness Protection Unit."

"Okay, so can you categorically reassure me that you have not divulged this location to anyone however much you may trust them?"

"Absolutely no one, sir, the protocols are very clear and I would never compromise a safe house location to anyone," said Perkins with growing indignation that his integrity was apparently being called into question.

"Good man," said Avery with a confirmatory pat on Perkins' shoulder. "Hopefully it's a false alarm but you understand we can't take any chances with this one which is why I had to come out myself."

"Yes sir," said Perkins, still not completely understanding the reason for the visit but relieved that he had apparently been exonerated from any wrongdoing.

"You had better introduce me to Mr McKenzie before I go so he knows he is getting premium treatment," said Avery, gesturing toward the stairs.

Perkins dutifully ascended the stairs with Avery following closely behind. When they reached the small first-floor landing area it occurred to Perkins that he didn't know which bedroom McKenzie had chosen to occupy but the sound of a television coming from the larger bedroom provided him with his best guess. Sure enough upon entering the room he saw McKenzie reclined on the double bed watching the television affixed to a bracket on the opposite wall. He had not heard the arrival of Avery or the brief conversation that had taken place downstairs so was surprised to see another man follow DC Perkins into the room. A cursory look in Avery's direction however allayed any fears that he had about the newcomer's arrival as it was clearly another cop; he had seen enough over the years to recognise the 'type' whether they were in uniform or not.

But as the younger familiar officer began to introduce his colleague, the older man did something very un-police like. The blade of the previously concealed knife was swiftly pulled across DC Perkins' throat, severing his carotid arteries and causing blood to splatter across the room. McKenzie felt some of the warm blood land on his face as recoiled in terror at the murderous act he had witnessed. The shock seemed to disable his voice as he struggled to sit up without the full co-operation of his flailing limbs whilst his eyes were firmly fixed on the assailant who was now pointing a handgun toward him.

Avery carefully stepped over the body of DC Perkins as he slowly approached the bed. He was smiling broadly which only added to the terror rising in McKenzie who now managed to utter some words that amounted to incoherent pleas for his life.

"If you want to live, Sean, you will do exactly as I say, do you understand?"

McKenzie nodded vigorously, not trusting his voice would convey a clear 'yes'.

"Excellent," said Avery, dropping the knife to the floor, leaving him one free hand. "Now, I want you to turn over, face away from me and put your hands behind your back because I am going to handcuff you. Nod if you understand."

McKenzie again nodded but he had no real comprehension of the instruction until Avery calmly repeated it. As he stared at the wall a few feet in front of him he heard the man walk closer and anticipated the familiar feel of cold steel enveloping his wrists. Instead the last feeling he had was a soft cushion being pressed to his head as Avery used it as a noise suppressant whilst despatching a bullet into Sean McKenzie's confused brain.

CHAPTER 62

It didn't take Avery long to wipe the bloodied knife and place it back into the holster sheath. He also replaced the gun back into its temporary position in his trouser waistband where it had been carried in the small of his back. His tightly fitted leather driving gloves were the only real bloodstained bits of clothing on his person but he would obviously discard everything when able. The only thing that had differed in reality from his earlier visualisation of the murders was the ineffectiveness of a cushion as an improvised silencer.

He quickly walked downstairs and left the cottage through the same door that he had entered a few minutes earlier. There was a satisfying click as the yale lock did its job securing the cottage and he walked quickly to the people carrier to collect his tracking device. The retrieval took him a bit longer than expected and he became aware that an elderly couple were now walking their dog past the property so he turned away from them and pretended his action was a tyre inspection. It was whilst looking away from the road that he saw the young boy standing at the open side gate with a football under his arm.

The boy had a puzzled expression but did not seem unduly alarmed by Avery's presence, who was acutely aware that the passing couple remained within audible range. He remained on his haunches as he engaged the boy in what he hoped was a friendly manner.

"Are you any good at fixing car tyres, son?" he called out.

The boy furrowed his brow as though making a consideration as to whether this was a serious request for help before regretfully shaking his head.

"What's your name?" asked Avery, trying to establish why a young boy should be in the grounds of a safe house.

"It's Cameron McKenzie, who are you?" came the reply.

Avery put his finger to his lips to signify discretion and then produced his police identification from his jacket pocket. Even from the distance between them the boy recognised the shiny metallic badge that adorned the warrant card holder and was delighted with the conspiratorial manner in which it was being displayed. He edged forward and looked at the car tyre to see if his limited knowledge of such things would be of any assistance but to him it appeared perfectly normal.

"I heard a loud bang," he said.

"Yes, that was me, I am afraid, the other policeman called me out here to fix this wheel but I think I made it worse," said Avery with a comic expression that made Cameron laugh.

"I think I am going to have to go back to the police station and get another one, do you want to come with me?"

The boy glanced nervously over his shoulder and Avery was quick to identify the dilemma Cameron was wrestling with.

"It's up to you but the other policeman said it would be okay and your uncle is snoring his head off upstairs."

"Have you got a police car?" he asked, still delighting in the mental image of his Uncle Sean snoring loudly.

"It's just a normal car but there are lots of police cars at the station, if you want we could bring one of them back?" suggested Avery, knowing the offer would seal the deal.

"With blue lights and siren?" asked Cameron.

"Yes and as a special treat as it's nearly Christmas you can operate them if you promise not to tell my boss."

"I promise," said Cameron, solemnly dropping his football to the ground to signify he was ready to go.

Avery extended his hand and led the boy towards his waiting car still not fully understanding why McKenzie's nephew had been at the house but recognising that leaving him there would in all probability cause an alarm to be prematurely raised. He was careful to avoid eye contact with the elderly couple whose progression past the property continued to be painfully slow despite the dog pulling impatiently on its lead. When satisfied that the boy had managed to correctly fasten his seatbelt he pulled slowly away and began to consider what to do next.

CHAPTER 63

Bare always found driving was a useful time to formulate his thoughts. The autopilot part of his brain was more than capable of dealing with the challenges of traffic allowing the remainder to process the myriad of other thoughts. He found himself approaching Avery's home address with nothing more than a notion that he wanted desperately to speak to the man about Robin's findings. He had always relied on his intuition when investigating crimes and he had an increasing feeling that things were being withheld which considering his personal involvement irked him greatly. He was disappointed to see an empty driveway at the address although it was probable that Avery was amongst the tiny minority who garaged their car.

It was of course equally likely that the man had taken the afternoon off to do something specific which would explain why he had not responded to the voicemail Bare had left him earlier, he belatedly considered. The sound of the ringing phone amplified through the hands-free system in his car curtailed further thought and he wondered if his arrival had led to coincidental contact from his boss. A check of the caller display, however, showed it to be Mary McKenzie and he considered how much of a regular occurrence this was going to be.

"Hello," he answered wearily, refraining from using names just in case someone else was using her phone.

"I am sorry to bother you again but I am worried about the boys," she said, wasting no time on extraneous detail.

"What's the problem now, Mary?"

"Well your boy came and picked them up but I have heard nothing from them since."

"What do you mean 'them'?" said Bare, picking up on the plural within her statement.

"The Witness Protection people said it was okay to take wee Cameron as well as Sean and I thought I would feel better with them both being looked after but I don't," she said.

"Well I am sure they are fine and if you have any concerns you really should use the contact number of the WPU, I have no idea where they have been taken, nobody does, which is why they will be safe," said Bare with growing frustration.

"I know exactly where they have been taken, place called Holstead," she replied.

"Mary how can you possibly know that? Has Sean been in contact because if he has he is jeopardising their safety," said Bare accusingly.

"No, there has been no contact but I just sort of found out," she said with hesitation, knowing that Bare was going to demand more detail.

"You sort of found out?" came the predictable reply.

"Sean gave Cameron his old phone because he got a new one, just to play games on, and I remembered I could track it so I had a look and they were in Holstead," she explained.

"Their phones should have been taken off them, you are going to have to ring the WPU and tell them, Mary, we shouldn't be having this conversation," said Bare, his voice now at least containing some empathy.

"Yes, okay, I am not used to putting my trust in cops," she explained.

"Well like I said, the lad who is with them is one of the good guys, they will be okay but you need to ring it in," replied Bare.

"Okay, but I thought they were just going to be taken to a safe place overnight, why would they be on the move again now?" she asked.

"What do you mean, Mary?" he said, feeling his heart begin to beat a little quicker.

"I am looking at the app now and they are driving towards the coast, why would they be changing places?"

"I don't know," was his honest reply as he started his car engine. "Tell me exactly where they are as I am not far from Holstead."

CHAPTER 64

As the text updates continued to arrive from Mary he managed to dial Sharon Brady's number whilst driving at an increasingly high speed. Still uncertain as to what was going on Bare was now relying heavily on his gut instinct and that was telling him something was seriously amiss. He swore aloud with frustration as his attempts to contact her were met with a persistent engaged tone. The fading afternoon light added to the oppressive feeling in the pit of his stomach as he made a reckless overtake to ensure the clear road ahead was commensurate with the speed of his vehicle.

His phone rang again and this time he saw it was Sharon Brady trying to contact him and he impatiently tapped the green call receive button.

"Where are you?" she hissed in a whisper. "I have been trying to ring you for ages but you are constantly engaged."

"I was on the phone and then trying to ring you. I need you to do me a big favour, Sharon," he began but before he could continue she interrupted him still using a whispered tone.

"Yeah, forget that. I am at the hospital, Seb, Jackanory has woken up and you are not going to believe this, the shit has hit the proverbial…" She said, barely able to contain the excitement of her recent discovery. "He has identified the man who stabbed him and he says it's—"

"Paul Avery," said Bare, finishing her sentence for her and leaving her shocked for the second time in as many minutes. "Look, Sharon, I don't know exactly what's going on but you need to contact WPU and get them to check Perkins is okay, I think the safe house where they had McKenzie has been compromised."

"What the fuck has that got to do with our Super being accused of stabbing someone? Where the hell are you, Seb?" she demanded.

Bare was about to answer part of her question when his phone flashed a warning that the battery was at a critically low level. Fearful that continued conversation would drain it completely he terminated the call and checked the latest of his many text messages from Mary which indicated a location which was now appearing static. Bare quickly punched in the coordinates into his sat nav as his phone rang again displaying Brady's number. As he pressed the receive button all the lights on the display disappeared and he realised he had no means of communicating with the outside world.

"Fuck, fuck, fuck," he said aloud but the only response was a robotic voice telling him he would arrive at his destination in sixteen minutes.

CHAPTER 65

"Why have we stopped here?" asked the boy as Avery applied the handbrake in the otherwise deserted clifftop car park.

"Because I used to come here a lot as a boy and I wanted to show you a really special secret place, Keith," said Avery, staring through the windscreen at the expanse of grey sea that stretched to the horizon.

"My name's not Keith, it's Cameron," reminded the boy.

"Well all good cops have a nickname so I am going to call you Keith," said Avery. "Come on, I have to show you the place before it gets dark."

The boy reluctantly got out of the car, doubting that the experience would match that of a promised ride in a police car and quietly followed the man who appeared to be searching for a remembered route.

'This way, Keith," he called, climbing over a stile that provided an exit from the car park and onto a narrow path that seemed to lead down from the cliff top. "It's not far."

Cameron sincerely hoped 'not far' was a truthful appraisal of the distance ahead and not merely a ploy used by adults to cajole their offspring along. He was feeling cold and hungry and if this is what police work entailed he would need to re-evaluate his career choices.

By contrast Avery was oblivious to the rapidly cooling air and had been transported back to his youth as he marvelled at the unchanged landscape around him. As he rounded a corner he saw that his destination was in sight, the familiar ledge where it had all began. The only issue he had was going to be how to reach it given that their approach had been from a different direction than it had been all those years ago. As he stood surveying the problem he was joined by the boy whose length of stride had caused him to fall behind and there had been no great enthusiasm to compensate by increasing his speed.

Avery pointed to the ledge and told Cameron they would have to leave the pathway and edge across carefully to it. The prospect of clambering across some slippery rocks in ever decreasing light did not enthuse the boy but he knew enough about male authority figures not to vocalise his protest so he followed the lead of the policeman. The pair made slow progress over the terrain with Avery more hampered by inappropriate formal footwear than he had anticipated. Such was their focus neither noticed the arrival of the second car in the car park above them.

Bare pulled alongside the parked vehicle wondering whether it was connected to his quest or just an indication of a hardy winter rambler nearby. He didn't recognise it as belonging to Avery which added to his indecision. A quick temperature check of the car's bonnet suggested it had arrived only a short time before him. He looked around to see if there was any obvious pedestrian route away from the car park and saw a wooden stile that afforded access to a footpath. Instead of climbing over it in the traditional way he used its height as a vantage point to see if he could see any signs of human movement. His initial focus was on the footpath that appeared to wind its way down to what he presumed was a beach area. Large parts of the path were camouflaged by foliage so it was possible persons were on it but invisible to him, he mused, undecided whether to keep observing or blindly follow the path himself. Then he heard the shout that diverted his gaze away from the defined route and onto the rougher ground below him.

"Wait for me!" the boy shouted again, unsure of his destination and not wanting to lose contact with his guide who was now several metres ahead of him.

The second shout allowed Bare to narrow down his area of scrutiny and he saw the silhouettes of a man and boy clambering across some rocks. Now knowing without hesitation he was in the right place he jumped down from the stile and ran in pursuit of the pair.

Avery reached the ledge first and made no effort to assist Cameron's final part of the journey, preferring to sit on the very edge with his legs gently swaying as he watched the waves crash into the rocks below. The late afternoon light was now causing the sea water to have an iridescent glow as it relentlessly swirled below his feet. He barely noticed the arrival of the boy despite his melodramatic announcement that was the 'furthest he had ever climbed in his life'.

Cameron, like his predecessor Keith all those years ago, was not unduly impressed with the 'special place' Avery had promised to show them and attempted the same ploy to encourage an early departure from it.

"I am really hungry, can we go to the police station now?" he said.

Avery ignored the question, preferring to use his own narrative.

"When I was younger I used to jump off here for a swim, it's a brilliant feeling."

With his back against the cliff wall Cameron leant forward very slightly to gauge the drop before exclaiming, "No way, that's such a big drop."

"Are you a good swimmer, Keith?" asked Avery.

"Yes, I have got my 10m certificate," came the proud reply.

"That's good then. Anyway if you are hungry we had better go and get some chips from the police station canteen before it shuts, help me up," said Avery, holding up his left hand above his head.

CHAPTER 66

Bare was once again formulating a plan as he moved steadily toward the ledge. He was close enough to see the adult figure was sitting on the edge and the child was standing behind him. Something about the pair's body language made him certain that he needed to intervene at the earliest opportunity so he shouted Avery's name.

The sound of the familiar voice shocked him and caused Avery to postpone his murderous intent and stare into the gloom to identify its origin. By now Bare was less than ten metres away and had managed to find a large flat rock that provided him with enough confidence to stand upright. It took a moment for Avery to scramble to his feet whilst regaining his composure at the unexpected interruption. Now ignoring the boy with him he looked across at his Detective Sergeant and shook his head slowly.

"Sebastian, I am seriously disappointed to see you here but a little bit impressed too," he said with a broad grin that made the scene even more surreal to Bare.

"It's over, let the boy go," said Bare with all the authority he could muster.

"Are you on your own or are the cavalry about to appear from over the hill?" enquired Avery as he placed a surreptitious hand on the boy's now trembling shoulder.

"The others are in the car park, we just want to end this without anyone getting hurt," said Bare, trying to maintain his composure in order to both bluff Avery and not further alarm Cameron who was now visibly shaking with an uncertain fear.

Avery studied Bare before making his own conclusion about the developing situation.

"Sebastian, we really should play poker sometime if your 'tells' are that transparent. I have a strong feeling that however you arrived here it was nothing to with a planned operational response. Honestly your maverick nature will be the death of you one day."

"Jackanory is awake and has named you, Paul, it's all over so just let the boy go and we can talk," said Bare, hoping that his revelation would cause Avery to understand the futility of his actions whatever they were.

"Don't tell me what to do and you call me 'sir', you insignificant piece of shit," snapped Avery as his grip tightened on the boy, making him cry.

"It's okay, Cameron, you are alright," called Bare with an increased fear that the boy's safety was far from assured.

"Okay, sir, you tell me what you want," said Bare, raising his hands in a placatory gesture.

With his free hand Avery retrieved the handgun from the small of his back and pointed it at Bare. Knowing that he only had one round of ammunition left he could ill afford to waste it so hoped that the menace of the gun's presence would do for now. The revelation about the awakening of the homeless one certainly now meant he would have no option but to flee and begin again elsewhere which had always been a contingency plan at various stages of his life.

"What I want, Sebastian, is for you to come and join Keith and me over here," Avery instructed and made a beckoning motion with the gun to emphasise his wish.

Bare recognised that compliance with the instruction would place him in a much more vulnerable position so attempted to stall for time.

"So are you being blackmailed like Morton was? We can still sort this," said Bare.

The question seemed to amuse Avery and he lowered the gun as his manic broad grin made an unwelcome reappearance.

"You really have no idea who I am or what I am capable of. I thought the super cop had worked it all out but you genuinely haven't got a clue, I take it all back about being impressed," said the contemptuous Avery.

"So tell me, sir," said Bare, moving forward a couple of steps.

"What would you like to know, Sebastian? Why I eliminated a crime family you spent years unsuccessfully pursuing or maybe you are just interested in something that happened closer to home?" said Avery, delighting in the rare opportunity to talk about his work.

The inference was not lost on Bare and his growing suspicion of Avery's involvement in Julia's death had now developed into an absolute certainty that he was staring directly at her killer.

"Why the hell would you do that to Julia?" he said.

Avery saw that Bare was slowly getting closer but made no mention of it as it was exactly what he wanted to happen. If the details of her death were what was required to bring him closer, then he was happy to provide them.

"Julia became a fascination to me, I think deep down she desired me so I paid her a visit when her husband was out misbehaving. And then I realised that long after the memory of seeing her lovely naked body faded, I could still feed off the pain I caused. Every time I saw your sad eyes at work and laugh quietly at your blissful ignorance it would be an exquisite echo."

Bare had never hated anyone more at that point in his life but his focus on the crying boy forced him to remain detached from his emotions.

"So what now?" he asked, having reached the ledge but standing in such a way that the majority of his body was shielded by rock preventing Avery from having a clear shot.

"Now somebody has to die, Sebastian, but I am going to give you the choice as to who. If you sacrifice yourself you have my word I will go and leave the boy here unharmed so he can tell the world what a hero you were. Otherwise Keith here is going for a swim and you can take your chances with me."

To reinforce his threat Avery forced the boy closer to the edge and the action caused some loose stones to disappear into the sea below, signalling the extent of the drop in store for Cameron.

"It's not much of a choice. What makes you think I would die to save a McKenzie? It doesn't have to be this way," called Bare.

"I don't think you could live with yourself knowing you could have saved a child. Think of it as payback for not being there to save your baby," said Avery.

"You bastard," said Bare, stepping out to allow Avery unrestricted sight of the man whose hands were up in surrender and was openly weeping.

Avery let go of Cameron using that hand under the other to steady his aim. As he squeezed the trigger he felt the double-handed push of the boy in his back. Bare felt the searing pain in his left shoulder at the same time he heard the explosion of the gun firing. The impact of the bullet caused him to step back but to his surprise he remained standing as he saw Avery stumble toward him. Bare instinctively presented a side profile and raised his right arm to fend off the flailing attack coming his way. Avery was already too close to be punched so Bare improvised with a forearm smash into his assailant's head causing both men to lose their balance. Both were perilously close to the edge but Bare reacted the quickest, allowing him to land one more blow before scrambling backwards to the comparative safety of the cliff wall where Cameron had been standing paralysed with fear. The anguished scream of Avery as he disappeared from view was a brief affirmation that the final blow had sent him spiralling backwards off the ledge and into the sea below.

The father and son slumped to the ground and held each other in a tight embrace with Bare no longer feeling the pain in his shoulder but grateful to hear the distant wail of approaching sirens. After a few precious minutes where no words were needed the pair got slowly to their feet and with meticulous care made their way back towards the car park. As they rejoined the coastal path and headed toward the large welcome party assembling in the car park Cameron tightly held Bare's hand.

"Will we get in trouble now?" asked the boy. "I only pushed him because he was going to hurt us."

Bare smiled at the personification of innocence alongside him.

"No, you were brilliant, I can't wait for you to join the police and be my partner."

"I am not sure my grandma wants me to though," said Cameron ruefully.

CHAPTER 67

It had been six months since Jackanory had experienced the freedom to walk in the fresh air. He had respectfully declined the offer of hostel accommodation and although he had grown used to the comfort of a bed he was actually looking forward to a night under the stars. It was of course early summer and he was determined to feel the sunlight on his face as he made his way slowly towards the town centre park, curious to know whether he would be reacquainted with some familiar faces or whether they had been replaced by people new to street life who he would have to take under his wing. He suspected the hospital staff had been overprotective of him, given the severity of his injury and lack of onward prospects. Eventually they had relented to his pleas to be released and conceded that physically he was probably now in the best shape he had been in for years. He would of course miss the regularity of meals and drinks but he suspected that the hospital canteen staff would remember him fondly should he ever feel the need to pop in for occasional sustenance.

He initially ignored the car that had slowed to his walking pace beside him but then he recognised the male voice that came from within it via the open window.

"Oi, I told you I would come and give you a lift into town," said the mildly rebuking Bare.

"And I told you I didn't need a lift. Typical bloody copper, never listens," snapped Jack but his smile betrayed the fact he was pleased to see the man who had been a fellow patient but then his most regular visitor in hospital.

Realising it was futile to insist he got into the car Bare parked it and joined the man on the roadside.

"So what's your doorway of choice tonight?" he asked.

"Don't know yet, been away for a while so probably lost my spot by now, but anywhere is better than that bloody hostel," said Jack and instinctively he touched his stomach.

"Yes, that was a bit insensitive of them to offer you a place back there," agreed Bare.

The police officer then took a key from his pocket and handed it to Jack who looked at it quizzically.

"Just in case the doorways are fully booked, it's a room at the Parkview guesthouse and it's yours for six months, breakfast included."

"That's the one run by Mrs Robinson where I used to pop in for a coffee," said Jack, showing understanding of the location but little else.

"Think of it as an informal gift from the Constabulary whilst your compensation claim gets sorted," said Bare.

"Thank you, I don't know what to say," mumbled Jack.

"Oh, and there is something else," said Bare, opening the boot of his car and retrieving a small holdall from within. "We had a whip round at the nick and bought you a bottle to mark your first night out and I used what was left over to get you a few items."

"Is it a decent brand?" said Jack, taking receipt of the zipped bag.

"Yes, I know you don't touch the cheap stuff. Good luck, Jack."

"Are you not going to join me for a drink then?" he replied with his broad piano key smile.

"Another time maybe, am off to Scotland for a family reunion."

Bare patted him on the back and in an instant had got back into his car and was gone.

Jack walked a few more yards until he arrived at an empty bench where he decided to stop partly for a rest but mostly to verify the bag contained the correct whisky. He unzipped the holdall and was pleased to see his favoured scotch inside. The bottle was resting on what appeared to be a number of full envelopes. After inspecting the contents of one, which caused Jack's eyes to open wide, he hurriedly replaced it in the bag amongst the other twenty-seven and clutching it tightly began walking towards his new home.

THE END

EPILOGUE

She stared at the reflections of the flashing Christmas lights on her window. The lashing rain caused the colours to somehow lose focus but she appeared transfixed nevertheless.

"I'm almost done, do you want me to make you a cup of tea before I go?" shouted her carer from the kitchen.

"No thank you, dear, I'll make one later," she replied, unwilling to exploit the services of someone she regarded more as a friend rather than an employee.

Within a few minutes she was alone in her house and she began gently sipping the tea made by her carer despite her earlier polite refusal. The television was on but she had little interest in the programme and lacked the inclination to search the channels for something better so she reached for her crossword puzzle book to make a further attempt at completing one she had started earlier.

The sudden knock at the rear door startled her and caused the spilt hot tea to scald her hand. Despite the painful burn she remained absolutely still, perplexed as to how someone had gained access to the small enclosed rear garden at the property. Any doubt as to whether she had misheard the origin of the knocking was removed when it sounded again, this time louder and more urgent.

With her composure slowly returning the eighty-two-year-old woman walked into the kitchen and was able to see the silhouette of her visitor throughout the partially paned door. Her curiosity as to the identity of the person outweighed any fears she had for her personal safety as she opened the door. She was met by the sight of a bloodied and soaking wet man who was holding on to the exterior kitchen wall, apparently unable to maintain his balance without its assistance. There was no exterior light so she struggled to identify the man in the darkness but as he started to speak a flicker of recognition crossed her face.

"Is that you, Michael?" she gasped as Paul Avery took the offer of her outstretched hand.

"Yes Mum, I have come home for Christmas," replied Avery and the pair fell into an embrace.

Printed in Great Britain
by Amazon

85871112R00159